SOPHIA & CAMERON

PALMERS OF COPPER CREEK BOOK TWO

NATALIE DEAN

DEDICATION

I'd like to dedicate this book to YOU! All of my wonderful readers that have been following my stories over the years.

I hope you're enjoying the Palmers of Copper Creek just as much as you've enjoyed the other close-knit families.

Thank you to my wonderful ARC Team who catches my errors for me and helps spread the word about my books.

And of course, I can't leave out my wonderful mother, son, sister, and Auntie. I love you all, and thank you for helping me make this happen.

Most of all, I thank God for blessing me on this endeavor.

ALSO BY NATALIE DEAN

CONTEMPORARY ROMANCE

Copper Creek Romances

BAKER BROTHERS OF COPPER CREEK

Copper Creek Romances Series 1

Cowboys & Protective Ways

Cowboys & Crushes

Cowboys & Christmas Kisses

Cowboys & Broken Hearts

Cowboys & Second Chances

Cowboys & Wedding Woes

Cowboys' Mom Finds Love

CALLAHANS OF COPPER CREEK

Copper Creek Romances Series 2

Making a Cowgirl

Marrying a Cowgirl

Christmas with a Cowgirl

Trusting a Cowgirl

Dating a Cowgirl

Catching a Cowgirl

Loving a Cowgirl

Marrying a Cowboy

KEAGANS OF COPPER CREEK

Copper Creek Romances Series 3

Some Cowboys are Off-Limits

Some Cowgirls Love Single Dads

Some Cowboys are Infuriating

Some Cowboys Don't Like City Girls

Some Cowboys Heal Broken Hearts

Some Cowgirls are Worth Protecting

Some Cowboys are Just Friends

Some Cowboys Fall for Hidden Stars

Some Cowboys Come Home for Christmas

Some Cowboys Brave the Flames

Some Cowboys Fight for Love

PALMERS OF COPPER CREEK

Copper Creek Romances Series 4

Mateo & Nicole

Sophia & Cameron

Roman & Olivia

Miller Family Saga

BROTHERS OF MILLER RANCH

Miller Family Saga Series 1

Her Second Chance Cowboy

Saving Her Cowboy

Her Rival Cowboy

Her Fake-Fiance Cowboy Protector

Taming Her Cowboy Billionaire

BROTHERS OF MILLER RANCH SERIES BUNDLE

MILLER BROTHERS OF TEXAS

Miller Family Saga Series 2

The New Cowboy at Miller Ranch

Humbling Her Cowboy

In Debt to the Cowboy

The Cowboy Falls for the Veterinarian

Almost Fired by the Cowboy

Faking a Date with Her Cowboy Boss

MILLER BROTHERS OF TEXAS SERIES BUNDLE

BRIDES OF MILLER RANCH, N.M.

Miller Family Saga Series 3

Cowgirl Fallin' for the Single Dad

Cowgirl Fallin' for the Ranch Hand

Cowgirl Fallin' for the Neighbor

Cowgirl Fallin' for the Miller Brother

Cowgirl Fallin' for Her Best Friend's Brother

Cowboy Fallin' in Love Again

BRIDES OF MILLER RANCH, N.M. SERIES BUNDLE

Though I try to keep this list updated in each book, you may also

visit my website nataliedeanbooks.com for the most up to date
information on my book list.

CONTENTS

1

Sophia Palmer

Five Years Earlier

"Oh, he's *cute.*"

Sophia swung her attention around to see where her hotel roommate was gesturing. Unsurprisingly, her eyes locked with the man she'd seen nearly everywhere she looked. He was tall—at least a good foot taller than her five-foot-three frame. The muscles in his arms bunched as he lifted a small glass of what was probably whiskey upward in a cheers motion before bringing it to his lips. His dirty blond hair was pulled back into a knot on his head, and he completed his hippie sort of look with ripped jeans and a T-shirt that showed off just how fit he was.

Yes. He was mouthwatering and the sort of guy a girl could melt into the floor over. Normally, he'd be the exact kind of guy she'd go for. He looked like he was up for a good time with no commitment.

But there was something in the way he smirked at her that unnerved Sophia to her very core. The hair on her arms rose as his unabashed stare continued to remain locked with her own.

Darcy leaned closer to Sophia, and her hot whisper brushed at her skin. "I think he's got a thing for you. I haven't seen him pay attention to any other girl."

Sophia rolled her eyes and turned her attention back to the crowd of mostly college-aged individuals who were dancing to the pop music playing at this particular bar. "Maybe he's looking at you."

From her periphery, Sophia noted the way Darcy tilted her head as she continued watching the stranger. "Nope," she said, popping the "p" as she turned to look at Sophia. "He's definitely into you. Maybe you should go ask him to dance."

"*Pass*," Sophia said with an exaggerated flourish. "We only came to this bar to have fun and maybe taste a few appetizers while we're at it." She winked and then jutted her chin at two men in hockey jerseys on the other side of the room. Now they were her type. Their lack of interest in anything serious couldn't have been more obvious.

With a wrinkle of her nose, Darcy shook her head. "Nah. The other guy is much better looking."

Yeah, the other guy was better-looking. He was probably charming as all get-out. And in thirty minutes, he could probably have her begging for something more. Sophia shook her head adamantly.

"How is he any different than the other *appetizers* you're interested in, huh?" Darcy pouted. Even though they'd only just met yesterday when they checked in for the horse breeding conference, she was already acting like they'd been friends forever. Darcy's face now blocked Sophia's view of the hockey hotties. With exaggerated movements, she darted her eyes in the direction of the man. When that didn't seem to work, she jerked her head in that direction. "Come on. He looks completely delicious."

Sophia took a sip of her drink and nodded. "Of course he does. But Mr. Manbun over there doesn't look like he wants a snack. He's here for the full five-course meal."

Darcy tossed back her head with a laugh. "Don't be ridiculous. He's harmless. Just look at him."

She had been looking at him. She'd looked at him in no less than four of the seven classes she'd attended at the conference. She'd looked at him the second he'd shown up at the bar. Sophia had looked at him so much that she could probably draw him from memory if she had the inclination. That wasn't the problem.

Mr. Manbun had looked right back.

Darcy groaned when she apparently realized she wasn't going to convince Sophia to take the steps necessary to hook the guy. If this was a simple catch-and-release, Sophia would have been on board. But something told her it wouldn't be that simple.

As if against her will, she let her eyes drift in his direction. But he wasn't there.

Sophia stiffened. Where had he gone? Had some other girl captured his attention? Probably. Darcy had said as much. The guy looked like a catch. Her focus bounced from dancer to dancer. Her eyes swept along the people milling at the bar.

"Looking for me?" a male voice said from behind her.

The hairs on the back of her neck lifted, and her heart stumbled. She didn't have to turn around to know who was behind her. His voice could only be described as a husky purr. Already, Sophia wanted to wrap herself up in the sensation of it.

Slowly, Sophia turned to face her visitor. She was forced to lift her chin in order to meet his eyes. Gorgeous blue eyes that looked almost gray peered down at her. One side of his mouth quirked upward in an infuriatingly handsome smirk. His facial scruff was neatly trimmed and only added to his allure.

No.

Sophia refused to allow this stranger to make her legs quake.

And yet, that smile drew her in.

It was all she could do to hide behind her own flirty and outgoing mask she wore when she was around any man.

She smiled and tilted her head as she narrowed her eyes. "Not hardly. I was trying to decide if it was time to leave. This place has lost its appeal. The music is giving me a headache."

For a moment he didn't move. But then he leaned in, and her breath caught in anticipation of his lips meeting hers. Why wasn't she backing away? Disappointingly, his face hovered just above her shoulder, his lips so close to her ear that she could feel the heat of his skin. "Liar," he whispered.

Goosebumps trailed along her arms despite the sticky heat coming from everyone dancing. Her head reared back, and she snorted, but no words formed on her lips.

His smile continued to stretch wider. Then he jerked his chin toward the dance floor. "Care to dance?"

Sophia arched a brow as she moistened her lips with a

flick of her tongue. Her throat had gone dry. This man had the ability to steal the air from the room, and it was making her feel lightheaded.

She was just about to accept his offer when someone bumped into her on their way to the bar. It knocked enough sense into her head to clear it. "Pass," she said with a smile of her own. Then she spun around, her black hair swishing over her shoulder.

There was no way she'd look back. She couldn't afford to. Whoever he was, he was trouble. She was only going to be in Texas for a week. She didn't have time for a distraction like Mr. Manbun. This time next week, she'd be back on her brother's ranch and the stranger staring holes into the back of her head would be a distant memory.

"This place is much better. I like the music, too, don't you?" Darcy scanned the room the second they entered the bar she'd picked out. The bass pumping through the speakers was more reminiscent of what she used to listen to when she was in high school, which meant the majority of the people here were likely closer to her age. There were a lot more men in cowboy hats, too, which meant there would likely be more country music played.

Here, she was in her element.

Sophia nodded and smiled broadly at her new friend. It was only her second night in Texas, but it promised to be fun. She looped her arm through Darcy's, and together they made their way to the dance floor.

It wasn't hard to get lost in the music. She could let loose her inhibitions. She could forget that she had responsibilities back home. But most of all, she could forget that less than a year ago, she'd had her heart broken by a boyfriend who couldn't keep his hands to himself. The worst part was that it had happened shortly after her brother had been cheated on by his fiancée. Sophia pushed those thoughts aside and focused on the present.

They danced for going on thirty minutes when Darcy hollered over the volume of the music that she was going to get a drink. Sophia nodded but opted to stay on the dance floor. A slower song started, and a man with dark hair and dark eyes grinned at her and raised his eyebrows.

She held out her hand, and he took it, placing it on his chest. He took her other one and placed it around the back of his neck.

They swayed, not bothering to tell each other their names or where they were from. Tonight was about fun— about being with someone who smelled good and who could guide her across the dance floor without promising her the world or begging her to offer the same.

When the dance was over, she was ready for her own drink.

"Wow, Soph. You really know how to pick them," Darcy said over the edge of her drink. Her eyes were wide, and they followed the handsome cowboy as he returned to his own group of friends.

Sophia shrugged as she requested a bottled water. Then she faced her friend. "As long as he can move and doesn't step on my toes, that's all I need."

"Then maybe you'd promise me your next dance?"

The scream that erupted from Sophia's throat at the sound of his voice was swallowed up by the start of another upbeat song.

Darcy muttered a curse, even though she wore a smile on her lips. Her eyes practically sparkled as she let her focus sweep from the top of the man's head to his feet and back to his face.

Sophia turned toward the intrusion with a hand on her hip. She arched a brow at Mr. Manbun. "No offense, but you don't look like you could keep up."

The second he flashed his smile at her, she got distracted. But it was his low, sultry voice that did her in entirely. "You never know until you give me a chance."

Darcy nudged her, causing Sophia to stumble forward a step. She nearly bumped into the handsome stranger.

She'd caught him staring at her at the conference again today. He'd kept his distance, not approaching her no matter how many times their eyes met. It was strange, to say the least. Sophia's eyes narrowed as she flapped her hand at her back to stop Darcy from insisting that she accept the stranger's request. "Are you stalking me?"

Mr. Manbun chuckled. "I wouldn't dream of it."

"Then how did you know I was here?"

His gaze shifted to Darcy. It was only for a split second, but it had been enough.

Sophia gasped and whipped her head around to stare at her friend. "You didn't," she hissed.

Darcy flushed and lifted a shoulder. Then she backed up a step.

"Oh, no, you don't." Sophia's hand shot out to reach for her friend, but at that same moment, a warm hand wrapped around her elbow. He spun her around to face him. "One dance, Red. That's all I ask."

"Red?" Sophia scoffed.

His eyes darted to the streak of red she had in her dark hair.

"Oh," she said. At least he wasn't asking for her name.

With a groan, she eyed him warily. "One dance."

"One dance," he agreed.

"Fine."

He tugged her to the dance floor. That was her first mistake.

Her handsome stranger could dance. And it wasn't just swaying side to side with the occasional twirl. This guy knew his stuff. He spun her around, dipped her, and moved her into steps she wouldn't have been able to keep up with if he wasn't holding her against him. One dance turned into another, then another and another. It didn't matter if the dance was slow or fast. He had moves.

Sophia lost track of time. It wasn't until the room had started to clear out that she realized how late it had gotten. She pulled away from him, feeling very much like Cinderella at the stroke of midnight as she hurried across the room.

He fell into step beside her easily enough. "I want to see you again."

She tossed him a smirk. "What happened to one dance?"

He pulled her to a stop, and his eyes drilled into her. "I think we both gave up on that request a few hours ago."

Sophia couldn't maintain the heat of his stare, even if she wanted to, and forced herself to look for Darcy. She hadn't seen her in a while.

"I think your friend went back."

She gasped with surprise and a moderate amount of betrayal. "What?"

He reached for her hand, and she stared down at it where he traced his thumb over her knuckles. "I want to see you again," he repeated softer. It was almost like he wanted to say something more, but he was holding back.

The temptation to agree to a date was almost too much to bear. But she managed.

Sophia pulled her hand from his and shook her head. She replaced her desire with her usual mask of flirtation. "No thanks." Then without giving him a second look, she hurried out the doors to catch a cab.

2

______

Cameron Walker

"It's been how many days? Five? And she's still turning you down. I don't know, man. The conference is going to be over in two days, and you're never going to see her again. Why even try?" Hugo asked.

Cameron fought the instinct to scowl at Hugo. They'd come to the conference together per their boss's request. According to Mr. Vernes, they needed the most up-to-date information when it came to breeding and raising horses. Cameron hadn't argued, but nothing would have prepared him for meeting Red. She hadn't told him her name, and while he was sure her companion would have told him if he'd asked, he was enjoying the chase far too much.

"At this rate, you might as well cut your losses. She probably lives across the country in some small town anyway. Even if she accepted a date with you, what would you do? Follow her like a lost puppy?" The guy was too good at reading people. One look at Cameron and Hugo shot up on his hotel bed, mouth gaping. "You can't be serious..." He shook his head. "Nope. Because that would make you crazy."

Cameron shrugged. "I don't know what to tell you."

"I get that you've been able to track her down every night this week. And heck, the fact that she was willing to dance with you says something. But Cam, you can't just drop everything for a girl you barely know."

"What can I say? When you know, you know." It wasn't just her looks, though Red's curves were captivating in their own right. She was smart, witty, and she had enough spunk to keep him on his toes. No one had ever held his attention like she did. And if his only shot to make her his was to follow her to her hometown and woo her, then that was what he'd do.

Hugo muttered a curse. "You're either crazy or in love."

Maybe it was a little bit of both. Cameron smirked at his friend. "Her friend gave me their hotel room number last night. It took a few free drinks, but I got it out of her. I'm going over there, and I'm not going to leave until she agrees to a date."

Hugo threw himself back on the bed with a sigh. "Good luck, man. You're gonna need it."

CAMERON BRUSHED his palms along the top of his head, ensuring his hair was still in place. Red's door stood directly in front of him. Everyone was taking their lunch break, and there was a chance that she wasn't even behind the barrier. Still, his heart pounded like he was here to get down on one knee.

Hugo was right. He had lost his mind. What intellectual person opened their heart to a stranger without even knowing her name? And yet it felt like he'd known her forever. Plenty of women had hit on him over the last five days. And he hadn't missed a single second of seeing Red's jealousy. After that first night, she'd practically laid claim on him. Who was he kidding? She had his heart, and she didn't even know it.

But with her consistently turning him down, he had every intention of milking that jealous side of her—mostly because he felt it too.

Any time a guy put his hands on her, the fury built within him. It took a great deal of control not to pull her off the dance floor so he could shield her from the eyes of every hot-blooded male in a hundred-mile radius.

Last night seemed to be the tipping point for her, though. She'd practically pushed a girl out of the way when "I Know She Ain't Ready" by Luke Combs came over the speakers. It had been the first dance they'd spent in each other's arms, and somehow it already felt like their song.

And when they'd danced to it last night, she'd avoided looking into his eyes so much he could tell she felt the same way.

Her words still rattled around in his head after he'd asked her out last night.

I don't do *dating.*

No matter how many times he'd tried to change her mind, she refused. Then she'd slipped away. Again.

Cameron rubbed his palms against his jeans and took in a deep breath, blowing it out through pursed lips. This might be his only shot. There was no telling when she planned to go back home. He lifted his fist and rapped his knuckles on the door.

Then he waited.

At first, he couldn't hear anything. But then he heard a faint voice before the handle clicked and the heavy door swung inward.

Red stared at him with wide eyes. "What are you doing here?" Almost immediately, she whipped her head around. "Darcy!"

He heard a faint giggle, then the words, "You might as well hear him out. He knows where we live—at least for the next couple of days."

Red groaned and dragged a hand down her face. "Whatever you want—"

"Go out with me."

Her eyes flicked up to meet his. Wariness flittered through her expression, and it threw him so off guard that he nearly didn't hear her next word. "Why?"

At her expectant expression, he cleared his throat. "You can't tell me you don't feel the spark we have. There's something here."

Red could have shut him down, but she didn't. Instead, she leaned against the doorjamb with folded arms, her toe the only thing keeping the door open. "One date?"

"One date." Okay, that was a lie. He fully intended on asking her out again for tomorrow, and at that point, he'd plan on getting enough information to start his plan in motion. He already knew he needed more of her. Two dates weren't going to be enough.

"Just do it," Darcy called. "You know you want to."

Red's cheeks flushed and she rolled her eyes. "Yeah, whatever."

Cameron straightened. "Tonight. Nine o'clock."

She lifted a brow. "*Nine*? What are you? A vampire?"

He chuckled. "Maybe you'll find out tonight."

WHEN CAMERON ARRIVED to pick up Red from her room, he laughed to see her wearing a short-sleeved sweater with a high neckline. It wasn't exactly a turtleneck, but it covered enough of her skin that it was clear she was teasing him.

She grinned right back, and the sparkle in that look alone set his whole world alight. She was breathtakingly beautiful. Her sage-colored shirt highlighted the green flecks in her deep hazel eyes. It was fitted and paired with jeans that showed off every one of her curves.

He reached for her hand. It was the most natural thing in the world, and he was pleased when she didn't pull away. With fingers laced together, they headed down the hall toward the elevator.

Everything was going his way. Mercifully, the sky was clear. The stars shone brighter than ever. Tonight, he was going to show her just how good they could be together.

Red already knew they were in sync when it came to the dance floor. But romance wasn't built purely on chemistry, even if they had it in spades.

"You going to tell me where we're going?"

He smirked at her. "Patience." Cameron opened the door of his rental truck for her and gestured for her to get inside. She watched him through the glass until he climbed behind the wheel.

"My brother would kill me if he knew I was going out with someone while I was here."

He arched a brow. "Protective or overbearing?"

She waved a dismissive hand. "Probably a little of both. He means well, but he feels like he's responsible for us since we moved away from home to run the ranch with him."

"Us?"

"My brothers and sisters."

"Big family, huh?" He couldn't say he had the same.

"Yeah. You?"

Cameron shook his head. "One brother."

"Sounds nice," she said.

He chuckled. "You can't say your big family is that bad. I can tell you love them."

She gave him a flat look. "Oh? How is that?"

"It's the way you talk about them."

Red scoffed. "I barely said anything about them. In fact, I even said your family situation sounded nice."

"But not better. And it was the tone of your voice. You care about your family." He could tell she was working at hiding the smile that threatened at her lips. The dimple in her chin deepened, and it was easily visible, even in the dark.

She blew out a breath and tucked her thick black hair behind her ears. "So where are we going?"

A laugh tugged from his chest. "You really don't like not knowing stuff, do you?"

She smirked. "And you must fancy yourself a mind reader."

"Maybe I am."

Her laughter was a boon to his soul. He liked this carefree side of her. There was the snarky, witty side of Red. And there was the genuine, happy side. He was certain there were even more that he'd have the pleasure of unveiling as time wore on.

When they pulled into some fairgrounds fifteen minutes later, she gave him a surprised look. "The fair. It can't be open much longer. It's getting late."

"We won't be here long."

Her eyes narrowed, and then she chuckled. "Well, if I had known that you were confident enough in your dating skills that you thought you could accomplish everything in an hour or less, I would have accepted your request sooner."

Cameron turned completely serious, leaned across the armrest that separated them and whispered, "Oh, what I plan for you is going to take much more than an hour. By the end of our date tonight, you're going to be begging me for part two tomorrow."

Her lips parted with surprise as her eyes searched his. Then she pulled back and smirked at him. "Good luck with that, mister."

"It's Cameron." He waited expectantly for her to offer her name.

She nibbled on her lower lip, then smiled, holding out her hand. "Nice to meet you, Cameron."

"Are you going to tell me your name? Or will I have to keep calling you Red?"

She wrinkled her nose, and he thought for a moment she'd give in. But then she smirked with a knowing look. "*If you convince me to go out with you tomorrow, I'll give it to you then.*"

He took her hand and shook it. "Deal." Then he lifted her hand to his lips and kissed it.

Her eyes rounded as large as saucers at the intimate

touch. But then she blinked and tugged her hand free from his grasp.

Cameron strode through the fair with purpose. True to Red's observation, the fair was closing up shop. They only had about thirty minutes before those in charge would be closing down the rides, and he needed to get Red there before that happened. He hadn't brought her here to take advantage of the empty fairgrounds. There was something else happening tonight that was sure to get her attention. When he stopped in front of the Ferris wheel, Red laughed.

"You brought me here to go on one ride?"

He grinned. "There's more to it than that." Cameron leaned in closer to her, reveling in the way her breathing hitched at the sudden movement. He whispered, "Have a little faith." With that, he took her hand and tugged her toward the ride. It didn't take long at all before they were at the top.

And it took even less time for Red to realize they weren't going to come back down for at least the next twenty minutes. Cameron had offered money to the guy operating the ride to close the gate and not allow new riders.

Red gave him a dirty look. "You can't hold me hostage, you know."

"That wasn't my plan, but maybe it should have been."

She rolled her eyes and folded her arms. "I told you. I don't do dating."

"Why is that?"

A lift of her shoulders was the only thing she offered him. "I just don't."

"Maybe you haven't met the right guy."

She lifted a brow. "And what? You think that's you?"

"I know it is."

She stilled before she laughed. "You're either the cockiest guy I've met or the most delusional." A huff left her chest. "Maybe both." Then she eyed him. "What are we doing up here, Cameron? You clearly have a plan. What is it?"

He studied her for a moment. Then he looked at his watch. "Two more minutes," he murmured.

"Two more minutes for what?"

He grinned, then glanced at his watch again. As soon as the clock ticked to nine-forty-two, he jerked his chin upward. "Look up."

Slowly, she lifted her gaze, then her eyes rounded and she gasped.

Glittering stars shot across the sky. The meteor shower would only last for a few minutes, but based on the way Red's mouth hung open, he knew he'd made the right decision in bringing her here. Luck was definitely on his side, and nothing proved it more than when she brought her eyes to meet his and leaned forward to capture his mouth with her own.

Talk about seeing stars.

3

———

Sophia grimaced when Darcy squealed. "It really wasn't that big of a deal."

"Not a big deal? Not a big *deal*? You *kissed* him."

"And you're too much of a hopeless romantic." Sophia laughed despite herself.

Darcy pushed off her bed. "And you're going out with him again tonight before we leave tomorrow. I can't believe it. Tell me you got his number."

Sophia shook her head even as a blush rose on her cheeks. Whether she wanted to admit it or not, that kiss had been a big deal. She only ever gave the men she went on dates with hugs—at least after Brent had broken her heart. The fact that she'd kissed him said more than she wanted to admit right now. "I told him that I'd give him my number if tonight's date went well."

"Do you know where he lives, at least?"

She shook her head again. "But who knows? I've never done long distance before." Her stomach swirled even as the pains from her past attempted to sour the fluttering warm feeling when she thought about Cameron.

Darcy squealed again. "This is so exciting. I can't believe it."

"Me neither," she mused, moving to the edge of her bed. "Am I crazy? I feel a little crazy."

Her friend shook her head. "Nope. This is special. I can feel it. That guy has been chasing you down since the moment he saw you."

Sophia chewed on her thumbnail and frowned. "I guess so. But it's not like he doesn't have a horde of girls trying to get his attention. I've seen them. And he smiles at them just like he smiles at me." Her second-guessing was coming back to bite her in the butt.

"Don't do that," Darcy warned.

She turned her focus to her friend. "Don't do what?"

"Don't brush off what's happening between the two of you. He doesn't smile at anyone the same way he smiles at you. And when you're dancing with other guys... I've seen the way he watches them—like he wants to shoot them with laser eyes or something."

Sophia snickered. "The feeling is mutual."

"Yeah," Darcy sighed. "I noticed that, too. You guys clearly want each other. You might as well run off to Vegas before you go home."

Sophia gasped and threw her pillow at Darcy. It whomped her in the face before dropping to the floor.

"Hey!" Darcy squawked. "Now, you've done it!"

For the next ten minutes, the sorriest excuse for a pillow fight commenced. By the end of it, they were both breathing hard and laughing. Sophia rolled over onto her side and peered at her friend. "Do you really think we could make it work?"

Darcy rolled over to face Sophia with a tired smile. "Yeah, I do. He's crazy about you."

Sophia fought the fear and anxiety that threatened to overcome her. If she were honest with herself, she'd have to admit that Cameron hadn't actually danced with anyone on all the nights they'd managed to meet up at the same place. Girls had flirted with him, but he hadn't danced with them. Maybe Darcy was right. Not every guy was like Brent.

Not every guy invited the touch of another woman he wasn't currently dating.

~

"You look *hot*! Cameron isn't going to know what to do with himself."

Sophia pulled her friend into a tight embrace and laughed. For the first time in a couple years, she was actually excited about going on a date. She'd only ever allowed herself one date with any guy after Brent. One date so she could get her social fix. But with Cameron? Something told her she'd finally reached a turning point. She was ready to open her heart to someone new. It felt like they were already something special.

She pulled back, her heart fluttering wildly as she grinned at her friend. She wouldn't go so far as to say they were officially dating, but there was a little voice in her heart that was telling her to just take that leap.

"Do you know what you're doing tonight?"

Sophia shook her head. "No. But I think we might be going dancing. That seems to be the best way we connect."

Darcy nodded. "The chemistry you guys have on the dance floor is out of this world."

Sophia glanced down at her watch. He wasn't going to be picking her up for another ten minutes, but with how antsy she was becoming, it was only a matter of time before she took off and bailed on him just to save herself from another heartache. Her nerves were getting the better of her, and the only person who would be able to help her was one floor down. "I think I'm going to surprise him and show up a little early."

"Go get it, girl," Darcy encouraged, shoving Sophia toward the door. "And don't forget to get his number."

Sophia smirked. "I won't."

She headed for the elevator and then pressed the button for the third floor. When the doors opened, she wandered down, watching the numbers increase. It looked like she'd have to turn the corner before she got to his hallway.

Rubbing her clammy hands against her legs, she willed her heart to slow down. She could do this. It was only the start of something. She didn't have to plan her entire future with this guy.

Even as that thought occurred to her, she already knew she was in too deep. Cameron was the first guy in years who had gotten past her defenses and made her feel like she was worth something. He'd been persistent, and there was just something indescribable about the way that made her feel. That was probably why it was so easy for her to get jealous. She knew what she'd be losing if he lost interest in her.

She turned the corner and stopped short. Her heart jumped into her throat as she caught sight of Cameron.

He wasn't alone.

And she was kissing him.

Sophia's hands balled into fists, and her whole body felt like it was vibrating with jealous, heartbreaking energy as she ducked back down the hallway at her back. The pain that shot through her chest was excruciating. How could she feel this hurt when she'd only known him for a week? They weren't even exclusive, and it felt like he'd ripped her heart from her chest and stomped on it.

Her breaths came out in sharp spurts. She should march right up to him and slap that pretty face. How dare he hurt her this way? He'd worked so hard to convince her to go out with him when he was seeing someone else, too. How many girls was he chasing?

She was going to be sick.

Her hands clutched at her midsection as she gulped in deep breaths. Then the fury overtook her pain, and she stormed toward the elevator. She didn't need this drama. She didn't need a man in her life. Brent had taught her that men couldn't be trusted, and Cameron's actions had put the nail so deep into the coffin there was no getting it loose.

And Darcy was right. Sophia looked hot tonight. She wasn't going to put her hard work to waste. She'd go dancing until her muscles ached and she left smelling like sweat and cologne.

Not even ten minutes after she arrived at the bar did her phone start vibrating. When she pulled it out, Darcy's number showed on the caller ID.

Sophia frowned. She hadn't told Darcy what had happened. The girl was too much of a romantic. It would break her heart, too. If Sophia answered the phone, she'd lose it. Her emotions were running hot, and she couldn't guarantee that she wouldn't cry on the spot.

She shook her head and shoved her phone into her back pocket.

"Everything good?"

She looked up into the deep brown eyes of a guy who was only about six inches taller than she was. He was handsome enough, but he didn't make her feel like Cameron did. Sophia smiled and swallowed hard. "Just peachy."

He jerked his chin toward the dance floor. "Wanna dance?"

"Love to." She moved with him toward the dance floor. He wasn't the first guy who asked her, and he wouldn't be the last. She'd spend the rest of the night doing her best to forget the guy who had managed to steal a piece of her heart that, up until tonight, hadn't been damaged beyond repair.

About an hour later, she felt his presence. She didn't know what it was about him that spoke to her soul, but the instant he stepped into the bar, the hair on her arms lifted and her heart stumbled. It was as if the universe was playing a cruel joke on her—pushing the two of them together when she didn't have anything left to give him.

She fought the urge to look in his direction. She wouldn't give him the chance to see just how much he'd hurt her. But somehow her eyes betrayed her, and they looked directly at him.

He stood several yards from where she danced with some guy. She wasn't going to waste her time learning their names. They were all the same. But they could make her forget the pain she felt for long enough to keep her distracted.

Cameron looked mad.

More than mad, he was furious. His hands were balled

into fists, and his stance told everyone to steer clear. It was probably the reason no girls were approaching him. He was too far away for her to see much more than that, so she glared right back and returned her focus to the guy who had her crushed up against his chest.

She could feel his eyes locked onto her no matter how much small talk she attempted to make with the guy she clung to. Part of her wanted Cameron to hurt just like she was, while the other part of her reveled in the knowledge that he was probably just jealous that she was here with someone else.

A blur came out of nowhere, and the guy she was dancing with was pushed off her. When her eyes focused on the reason, she gasped. "Cameron!"

He whirled on her after telling the guy to beat it. "What are you doing, Red?" he demanded.

She folded her arms. "That's not my name."

Cameron stepped into her space. "So, tell me what it is," he snarled with exasperation.

"No."

His brows shot up. "Seriously?" He huffed out an angry laugh and pinched the bridge of his nose. "So you finally agree to go out with me, then ditch me. Was this all a game?"

"You tell me," she snapped.

"What is that supposed to mean?" he demanded.

Before she could respond, a deep voice spoke behind her. "Is there a problem here?"

"No—"

"Yes, actually, there is." She turned to find a guy with dark hair and dark eyes. He was cute enough and almost as tall as Cameron. They were eyeing each other like they were ready to start the next big war. She put on her best flirtatious smile. "Can we get out of here?"

"*Red*—"

She didn't bother looking at him as she reached out and touched the stranger's upper arm with a trace of her finger. "I could really go for some ice cream. What do you say?"

He smiled down at her and draped his arm around her shoulder, then led her away from Cameron and the wreckage he'd been responsible for.

4

____

Cameron

Present Day

"*T*hat's *not* my name."

Cameron smirked, hands shoved in his pockets. At first, he thought he was seeing a ghost. He'd been busy settling in the last couple of days, but he'd thought he'd seen someone who looked exactly like Red last night.

Apparently, his eyes hadn't been playing tricks on him.

"Will you wipe that stupid grin off your face?" she snapped.

"Not until you tell me your name." He glanced around the immediate area. "So, are you working here? Friends with the owners?" He'd spent the last five years being furious with this woman. Yes, the anger was still buried deep, but right now, all he could think was that he'd finally found her.

She was so close that he could smell her light perfume scent.

Her cheeks were flushed beautifully. The dimple in her chin was more pronounced with the frustrated set of her jaw. His elation was bound to wear off, but for now he was going to indulge in it. Maybe later he'd get his own form of payback.

"This is my *home*," she gritted out through clenched teeth. "And you need to leave."

Home?

So, this was where she'd been hiding all these years. He'd done what he told Hugo and left his job after meeting Red. He'd made it his mission to find her and that meant becoming the best at what he did. Contracts with some of the most prestigious ranches across the country had him traveling from state to state, which gave him a lot of opportunities to look for her.

Who knew that agreeing to a year-long contract with Mateo Palmer would grant him his greatest wish. He leaned in closer to her, his smile growing. "You're Mateo's sister."

She stiffened. That was all the answer he needed.

"So, Red. Are you going to tell me your name, or do I have to ask around? I'm sure I could find someone here who knows you."

Her jaw tightened further before she opened her mouth to speak. Unfortunately, they were interrupted.

"Oh, good. You've met *Sophia*."

Sophia's eyes rounded briefly, and then her glower returned when Cameron smirked at her and mouthed her name. Then he turned to face Mateo. "Yes. We were just getting to know each other. Isn't that right, Sophia?"

He didn't miss the way her hands flexed and clenched

several more times. She shifted her weight from one foot to the other, and he itched to reach out and take her hand to prevent her from bolting.

She wouldn't go far. This was her home. He'd finally found her, and there was nothing she could do about it.

There was so much lost time to make up for. In five years, not one woman had managed to draw his attention like Sophia had. She looked just as good as he remembered, better, even. Her hair was still medium length, but she'd added more streaks of red to her hair. The fire in her eyes was a change.

Cameron rocked back on his heels as he swung his focus to Mateo. He'd been told that he'd be working closely with Mateo's sister, as she was the one who oversaw the horses. He never dreamed that person would be the woman who got away.

Sophia spun toward her brother and opened her mouth, but Mateo cut her off. There was a woman and a child at his side, and he brought the woman's left hand forward.

Sophia's eyes widened, and the fury that had been lingering in her eyes faded away. She let out an excited squeal and pulled the woman into her arms. "I can't believe he finally did it!" She shot a firm look at her brother, to which Mateo just chuckled. That was all it took for Cameron to be forgotten.

That was fine. Cameron didn't need to be swept up in a celebration that he wasn't invited to. He stepped back slowly, withdrawing into the crowd of people who were mingling. It didn't take long for most of the people around them to get wind of the engagement and crowd the happy couple. Apparently, this union had been a long time coming.

Cameron watched from the outside. He'd always been an

outsider with how much he'd traveled. But now that he'd found her, that was going to change. With everyone's attention shifted to Mateo and his bride-to-be, Cameron permitted himself to watch Red.

Here, she was in her element. He could see bits and pieces of the woman he'd met in Texas, but the woman standing on the other side of the yard didn't feel the need to have her guard up. She was relaxed and carefree.

And man, if that didn't make him want her even more.

But he couldn't get ahead of himself. If Hugo were here, he'd be reminding Cameron that just because he'd found Red, he didn't need to go in with guns blazing. The progress he'd made with her during that week had disappeared.

How many times had Hugo told him that he needed to let her go? That her behavior on that last night indicated exactly how she felt.

The problem was that Hugo hadn't been there. He hadn't seen the flicker of pain and fear in Red's eyes. He hadn't felt the heartache.

Red covered it well enough, but Cameron had noticed all the same. The woman standing among her friends and family was hiding something, and Cameron was going to unearth it before he made her fall in love with him.

The sting of betrayal that had followed him these past five years flickered to life when Sophia moved to speak to someone.

Not just any someone.

A man.

Worse, the guy was Cameron's supervisor of sorts. At least he was in charge of the wranglers. With Cameron's contract, he didn't exactly report to anyone but Mateo.

She smiled with those pretty eyes up at that cowboy like he was the moon and stars themselves.

Dang it all.

Cameron's hand curled into a fist as all the pain came whooshing back with a vengeance. He knew it was possible that she'd found someone else. It was a strong possibility, actually. With the more time that had passed, he'd assumed the worst.

He'd even had nightmares where he'd finally found her, and she had a husband and kids.

But she didn't have a ring.

So that guy who was smiling down at her wasn't a husband or a fiancé. A boyfriend maybe? He wasn't touching her. They weren't holding hands. Who was he to her? Cameron took a step forward, but a deep voice stopped him in his tracks.

"He's taken."

Cameron stiffened before turning his focus to the man at his side. He looked familiar. Same dark hair, same tanned skin, and same dark eyes as Mateo. There was no denying that the two of them were related.

Where Mateo sported some facial hair, this version was clean-shaven. He was probably a couple inches shorter than his brother, too. The smirk that filled his face was more carefree than Mateo's as well.

With narrowed eyes, Cameron folded his arms. "Who?"

"The guy who's talking to my sister. He's actually married to my cousin."

Cameron blinked and swung his attention to the man again, only now, he had a girl curled into his side.

"His name is Daniel."

"I seem to recall that's what he said his name was," Cameron mused.

The man beside him gave him a cheeky grin—one that made Cameron instantly like him. He jutted his chin toward the group. "So, you want to tell me what is going on between you and my sister?"

Cameron smirked. "What would the fun in that be?"

The cowboy shrugged. "Maybe I could help."

"I doubt that." Cameron chuckled. "And even if you could, I work alone."

He laughed with a shake of his head. "Your funeral." He shoved out his hand. "I'm Roman. And you are?"

"Cameron." They clasped hands with a firm shake. Cameron drew his attention to the woman who still held his heart no matter how many times Hugo had tried to convince him to walk away.

"Is she dating anyone?"

Roman arched a brow. "I could tell you, but what would the fun in that be?"

Cameron chuckled. "Touché"

They stood side by side, watching the crowd of people slowly disperse. Roman wasn't going to offer any more information, and that was just fine by him. Cameron didn't need anyone helping him win Red over. He'd done it once, and he'd do it again.

Mateo got up on a picnic table and held his hands to either side of his mouth. "Let's get this party started."

Somewhere, someone started music on a speaker. Hollers and whoops filled the air. This man knew how to bring people together. He was charismatic, and the way he talked about his dreams was infectious. That attitude was the biggest reason for Cameron agreeing to such a long contractual period. Normally, he'd sign on for a breeding season, but he'd never stay long enough to see the fruits of his labor. Mateo demanded more, and Cameron had been swept up with Mateo's flowery words and expectations for the future.

The universe had finally answered his prayers, and he'd die before he didn't take this new opportunity by the horns.

At some point, Roman slipped off to chat with others at this event. Sophia glanced in his direction a few times, her eyes narrowed each time.

And whenever he caught her stare, he winked at her.

The motion seemed to set her off like a firecracker because she immediately tore her attention away from him. But the last time he winked, she deliberately moved over to a different cowboy.

Cameron had seen the guy around. He didn't look like Roman or Mateo, so he probably wasn't family.

Sophia reached for his upper arm and squeezed as she leaned in to say something to him. The cowboy laughed.

Definitely not family.

Something like a growl reverberated in his chest, and he strode forward with no thought to the consequences of his actions. It took no time at all to reach Sophia's side and less time to decide what he was going to do with her.

He grasped her elbow gently but firmly at the same time as he tugged her away from the guy she was shamelessly flirting with.

Her gasp was quickly followed by sounds of indignation as she attempted to pull away from him—only, he wasn't going to let that happen. Cameron escorted her across the yard to a quieter space beneath a tree where they could be shaded by the boughs overhead. Only then did he allow her to yank her arm free of him.

"What do you think you're doing?" she snarled.

What *was* he doing?

Right now, he had no claim on her. They weren't together. She'd made that clear five years ago. Fury licked at his insides, growing with more force. He deserved an explanation. She owed him that much. "What are *you* doing, Red?" His question burst from his throat in a heated breath. "You were all over that guy."

Her brows shot up, and she laughed.

She actually laughed.

It wasn't the sweet sound he'd grown accustomed to when she'd flirted with him in Texas. This one was poisoned with bitterness that almost made him feel as though she'd slapped him.

"I can't believe you right now. Seriously?"

He ground his jaw tight, waiting for an explanation, however unreasonable it was for him to want it.

Her eyes flicked between his, studying him before she shook her head with what could only be called disdain. She moved far too quickly for him to be able to catch her from darting away from him. He'd lost his chance to ask her what had happened. This had been his chance to demand answers, and he'd squandered it because of his own jealousy.

Cameron watched her go, his stomach sinking. He dragged a hand down his face. This was going to be harder than he thought. She clearly despised him.

5

———

"**W**hat have you done?" Sophia demanded.

Mateo turned from his conversation with Daniel, confusion marring his happy face. He glanced over at Daniel, who chuckled and withdrew, leaving them alone.

Sophia popped her hip, her arms crossed, an expectant glower drilling into the side of her brother's head.

"You're going to have to be a little more clear. I thought you wanted me to propose to Nikki. You said yourself that she's not—"

Tossing her head back with a groan, Sophia shut her eyes and focused on her breathing. "This has nothing to do with the engagement." She brought her focus to her brother, heat searing her whole body. She could feel Cameron's eyes on her.

The worst part was that he still affected her the same way

he had five years ago. The prickling of the hair on the back of her neck. The way her body reacted to his touch. She could sense him even if he was yards away.

He'd changed—matured some. His hair was different—cut in a style that was effortlessly mussed but probably took more time than it was worth. He still wore his facial hair neatly trimmed. And his clothing choice reflected years of working on ranches rather than the hippy look he'd favored.

He was mouthwatering gorgeous, and the jerk knew it.

This was bad.

So bad.

"Then what are you talking about?" Mateo demanded, yanking her to the present.

Her eyes cut to Cameron as if against her will.

Yup. He was staring right at her. It was a steady sort of stare—one that made her feel like he could see inside her soul and knew exactly how she was feeling.

The heat in her cheeks intensified, and try as she might, she couldn't shove those feelings aside. "Cameron," she spit. "What is he doing here?"

Her brother arched a single brow. For a moment she could see the cogs in his big, dumb head whirring, then suddenly a knowing smile spread across his face. "Do you know him from somewhere?"

Her mouth dropped open and that heat in her cheeks became even more prevalent. "I don't—we haven't—*no*. I *don't* know him." At least that much was true. She had thought she had known the kind of character Cameron had, but she'd been wrong. He had been hiding his own philandering ways from her. Of course she should have known better. She'd seen the way girls flocked to him. And he'd been good.

So good.

He'd known the right words to say to get past her defenses. He'd made her feel like she was the only girl in the room.

Then he'd stolen that feeling away.

Tears bit at the back of her eyes and she squeezed her arms tighter across her chest. "What is he doing here?" she repeated.

"He's working. Just like the rest of the guys."

Her brows rose. "What? No. You can't let him work here, Mateo. You have to fire him."

Her brother lifted both hands with his shoulders. "No can do, sis. He works via contract. We signed a contract for him to work here for the next year with the possibility of extending—though he said that's usually uncommon. He gets booked out. He's that good."

Well, this was just great. Her brother had a man-crush on Cameron.

It wasn't fair!

"Well, you're going to have to tell him to leave me alone—"

"Sophia, is there something you're not telling me? Because it really does sound like you know him."

She pressed her lips together in a tight line. She hadn't told anyone what had happened with Brent because Mateo had been dealing with his break-up with Caroline. Besides, her brothers would have gone out and taught her ex-boyfriend a lesson, and she knew better than to let that happen. After she'd let Cameron get past her defenses, she'd kept the whole ordeal secret because that one had been on her.

She'd been the one who allowed herself to believe that

building a relationship with a guy she'd just met was possible.

Turning away from him and avoiding the stare of the man they were speaking about, she shrugged. "We might have met when I went to Texas five years ago. He didn't make the best first impression."

"Really? Because he comes highly recommended. You don't know how hard it was for me to get a meeting with him."

Sophia peeked at Mateo with a frown. He was glancing over at Cameron, who was now paying attention to something else. He probably knew they were talking about him. If he came so highly recommended, then he probably had other clients he could work with. Why couldn't he just break the contract and leave?

She swung her focus to her brother once more. To his credit, her brother looked concerned—like he was torn between making her happy and doing what he thought was best for the ranch. Ugh!

Guilt rumbled in her gut, and she knew she wasn't going to be able to force Mateo to give up on something he wanted. He'd already sacrificed so much. His life was finally coming together, and if working with Cameron was the next step he wanted to take place, then so be it.

She sighed, pulling Mateo's attention. "Fine. Whatever. Let him stay for the duration of the contract. What is it he does, exactly?"

"He specializes in breeding. The stronger the bloodlines, the better. He knows his stuff, Sophia. He can help create excellent racehorses, or work horses. The last couple of people he's worked for swear by him."

Sophia groaned again. "And that means he has to work with me since I'm in charge of our horses."

Slowly, Mateo nodded, and that smirk returned to his face.

What she wouldn't give to turn back time to stop this from happening. Seeing Cameron again had opened up some deep wounds. She'd managed to enjoy her life boyfriend-free since he'd ripped her heart out, and she planned on it staying that way. Despite not knowing Cameron well, she knew he was one of those guys who enjoyed the chase. He was unapologetically jealous and cocky to boot. He probably just didn't like the fact that she'd been the one to see through his charade before he could land whatever prize he'd been after.

Well, he'd just have to live with never adding her to his tally.

"Whatever. He's only here for a year, right?" And he'd be an idiot to chase after his boss's sister, so she should be safe.

Mateo nodded. "Just a year."

She blew out a sharp breath. "You owe me."

Sophia made sure to wear her tightest jeans and a shirt that showed a little more skin than she usually did when she worked. If she had to work alongside the man who broke her heart, the least he deserved was to see just what he had missed out on.

Her shirt was a button-up vest with no sleeves, and it rode up a little to show about an inch of her midriff. It was cute and made her feel like she could conquer the world.

She reached for her leather gloves and her brown Stetson, then headed out to the barn.

Cameron specialized in breeding, so she didn't know what he'd be doing besides picking what stallion got to breed with what mare. That didn't seem like much of a career, and based on the way her brother had described it, Cameron was getting paid top dollar just to make decisions.

Why couldn't Mateo trust her to do that job? She'd known that he wanted to start a breeding program for the horses. They were already the top brand when it came to breeding working dogs, and he'd said it shouldn't be too much different to add another animal to the list.

He'd said as much when he returned from an auction last summer. He'd been in a flurry of excitement, and that probably should have been the first indication that he was going to turn her life upside down.

Yes, she should have definitely known.

She strode out to the barn with her head held high. It didn't matter when Cameron planned to show up; he wasn't going to get in her way when it came to her caring for her babies. The horses were her responsibility, and she was good at it.

Sophia entered the barn and practically stumbled to a stop. Cameron was already in the dimly lit barn. It was too early for someone like him to be working. At least that was what she'd told herself.

But she'd been wrong.

Ugh!

Sophia stormed toward him. There wasn't a chance that he hadn't heard her arrival. Even though he hadn't turned to look in her direction, he was just as aware of her as she was of him. She knew it in her bones.

Before she got within ten feet of him, he drawled, "Good morning, Red."

"*Don't* call me that."

He peeked at her out of the corner of his eye with a mischievous smirk. "Seeing as that's what I've called you for the last five years, it's going to be a hard habit to break."

"Tough! You're going to have to figure it out!"

He chuckled, and the sound was like sunshine on her skin after the storm clouds had moved out. Why did he have to be so irresistible? He was a flirt—a guy who manipulated the feelings of women. There was a fine line between being a flirt who was open about not wanting anything serious and a flirt who made someone believe there could be more.

Heat seared her cheeks at the memories of their past. She'd told him she didn't want to date. She'd been upfront about it from the get-go. But he'd weaseled into her heart in a matter of days and made her want more.

He was the devil in disguise, and she wasn't going to let him manipulate her a second time. "What are you even doing in here this early? These horses aren't your concern."

Cameron arched a brow as he glanced up from the clipboard she'd only just noticed he had in his hands. "I'm sorry, but what exactly do you think it is I do?"

"You pick which horses get to breed with which horses." She said it with a matter-of-fact tone that she hoped left nothing to the imagination. His job was ridiculous. They didn't need him.

He tucked his clipboard under his arm as he folded them across his chest. "It's that simple, huh?"

"Isn't it?"

The smirk he gave her had her faltering. He took a step toward her, and she fought the instinct to take a step backward. Her eyes dipped from his eyes to his lips, and the memory of their kiss sent waves of electricity rippling under her skin. She swallowed hard and forced herself to focus.

"Yes." That one word sounded less confident than she'd wanted it to be.

"You know what I think, Red? I think you need to put your nose in a book. See what it takes to have my job before you come marching in here telling me how to do it right."

Her flush intensified, but whether by his low, husky tone, his proximity, or the fact that he'd put her in her place, she couldn't be certain. Her mouth went dry, and she fought for something intelligent to shoot back at him. Unfortunately, it appeared the last of her brain cells had chosen now to disappear.

"Hey, Sophia. We still on for that date tonight?"

She stiffened. Cameron's eyes left hers and whipped to the interruption with mild irritation. The spell broken, she exhaled and took a step back from the man who had her locked in his sights. Her legs shook as she took the steps toward the cowboy, who was oblivious to the tension in the barn as he retrieved a saddle. He had a boyish charm about him that was so different from the searing magnetism of the man who was now at her back.

Sophia reached out and touched Ryan's upper arm. She gave it a gentle squeeze as she lowered her voice to a seductive purr. "I wouldn't miss it for the world." She'd leaned in close but not enough to brush her lips to his cheek. Her ears were attuned to the man bristling at her back, and she realized something.

He was jealous.

Good. He'd broken her heart. All was fair in love and war, after all.

$$6$$

Cameron

Cameron clenched and flexed his hand as he watched Sophia's demeanor shift like she'd flipped a light switch. One second, she'd been antagonistic, and the next, she was flirting like her life depended on it.

Those smiles, those fluttering lashes, they belonged to him. He and Sophia were inevitable. She just wasn't ready to accept that quite yet. It had taken everything in his power not to march over to that Ryan guy and tell him to beat it. Sophia's heart belonged to him. He was sure of it. What he'd witnessed had been fake. So fake that he couldn't help but compare it to the way she'd been with him on their first date.

When Ryan left the building, Sophia was once again alone with him, and he could breathe again. She turned to face him, and the smirk on her face was nothing if not irritating. She'd known what she was doing. She was goading him.

Well, he wasn't going to let her see that she'd affected him.

He jerked his chin toward the horses. "As I was saying, if you think my job is just matchmaking, then you're sorely mistaken. What I do is more nuanced than that. My responsibility encompasses the entire care of the broodmares. I dictate what they eat, how they exercise, and even how often they get brushed down. My job is to make sure they're in prime condition for gestation.

Cameron studied her, watching as the realization dawned on her. He'd practically taken over her job. If she was overseeing the care of these animals, he had veto power. Her cheeks colored deeply, and he fought a laugh. If she thought spending time with him today was going to be hard, how could she deal with the repercussions of them working elbow to elbow for the next year?

Her mouth fell open, and she shook her head. "No. That's not right. It's my job to take care of these horses."

He shrugged, pulling his clipboard out and going over the notes he'd already taken since he'd moved in. "Sorry to break it to you, Red, but the contract has already been signed."

She let out a huff and stormed from the building out into the morning light. Cameron chuckled again. Five years ago, she'd strung him along and made him believe they could be something more. She'd agreed to their date, and then she had bailed on him only to leave with another guy. It might not be right for him to enjoy the fury that he saw sparking in her eyes, but he couldn't say he didn't relish seeing her upset after what she'd put him through.

One of these days, he was going to get an answer as to why she thought she could just desert him like that. What reason did she have to cause that sort of pain? If she wasn't ready for a relationship, she could have said it to his face.

But she had.

He grimaced. Yes, she'd told him she didn't do dating, but he'd convinced her to take down those walls. So why shouldn't he feel betrayed? It didn't matter that they hadn't known each other that well. Nor had it mattered that they'd just met. He knew from the moment he'd seen her that she belonged with him.

Which was why he would revel in the time he had with her. Eventually, she'd see that they were inevitable, and she'd finally accept it.

The first couple of weeks were torture. Well, not in the traditional sense. Sophia either avoided him or refused to speak to him about anything but work. Whenever another guy came within a couple feet of her, she'd flash him that irresistible smile and talk to him like he was the sun and the moon themselves.

Cameron was going to have to find a dentist with how often he ground his teeth at the interactions. At least they weren't as intimate as that first one had been. She hadn't touched them or kissed their cheeks. Still, he hated that she saved all her sweet smiles for men who didn't deserve it.

Today was no different. Some guy named Jason brought her out a water bottle from the building with the cafeteria. She thanked him with a hug that lasted two seconds too long.

Cameron narrowed his eyes on the man as he hustled back to his post. It almost looked like the hug had surprised Jason, but he hadn't pushed her away, so what did Cameron know? After the guy was safely away behind closed doors,

Cameron marched over to where Sophia was brushing down one of the chestnut-colored horses.

She hummed softly to herself but stopped when his shadow fell over her shoulder and onto the horse before her. She stilled her work, then glanced over at him. "Is there something I can do for you?"

He flexed his hand. "Why are you doing that?"

Her eyes widened with what she probably thought looked like innocence, but he knew better. "What? You told me you wanted them all brushed, and since most of the guys are on lunch break—"

"You know very well what I'm talking about. Why are you trying to irritate me by flirting with every man who comes within spitting distance of you?"

She snickered, and the sound was like music to his ears despite the reason for her laughter. "I'm not flirting with every guy."

"Yes, you are."

Turning, Sophia crossed her arms and arched a brow. "Sounds like you've been spying on me."

He took another step toward her. "It's not spying if you're doing it right in front of my face."

"Am I?" she sang like she didn't know exactly what she'd been doing.

Cameron crowded in on her, his face within inches of her own. The smug look on her face faded and desire flickered in her eyes. He could feel the warmth of her breath as she exhaled a sharp breath. When he reached up and tucked a strand of hair behind her ear, she shivered. "When are you going to accept that there is something between us?"

Just like that, the desire faded, and her eyes narrowed. She placed both hands against his chest and gave him a little shove. "You're so full of yourself, you know that? Maybe you need to accept that you're not irresistible. Not every girl is going to fall at your feet and beg for you to take them on a date." With that, she stormed away from him and headed for the house.

He wasn't allowed to be in the house. His home was the wranglers' cabin, and if Mateo got even a whiff that Cameron had a thing for Sophia, there was no telling what would happen. He hadn't explicitly said that Cameron wasn't allowed to date Sophia, but he didn't seem like the kind of boss who would approve of such a thing.

There would be no chasing after Sophia. If she didn't want to speak to him, all she had to do was hide away in her home.

He let out a growl. Cameron must have been a little crazy for thinking that being here with Sophia would give him a chance to win her over, because every time he interacted with her, it ended badly.

A huff of a sigh escaped his chest, and he turned back to the horse that Sophia had been brushing down. A chuckle filtered to him at his back. It was low and so completely full of amusement that it was impossible to ignore.

Cameron turned to face the intrusion, finding a man who couldn't have looked more like Mateo if he'd tried. Clearly, they were brothers. The only difference was the lack of facial hair. Cameron grunted, turning his back on the man. "Did you need something?"

The man chuckled again. From what Cameron remembered, his name was either Roman or Marcus. They didn't interact as much as Cameron interacted with Mateo, but that was to be expected since he was the boss.

When Sophia's brother didn't respond, Cameron paused and turned to face him. "What do you need?"

The man shrugged.

Cameron narrowed his eyes. "Look, if you want to say something, you might as well say it. I'm busy, and I don't have time for someone who's just going to hover."

The man chuckled again. "All I was gonna say was not to take it personal."

Arching a brow, Cameron stared at the guy expectantly.

"Sophia. She doesn't date."

"So I've heard," Cameron muttered dryly.

"Yeah. Don't let it bother you if she's flirting with other guys. It's not you. It's her."

"Why is that?" he asked. Sophia didn't seem inclined to say anything to him about this. He had a feeling she would rather poke her eye out with a piece of straw than discuss how she felt about dating.

The guy shrugged again. "Beats me. All I know is that I've never seen a guy around here twice. If she goes out with you once, she's done."

Was that why she didn't want to go on that second date? Had she been scared?

No. He refused to believe that. The way she had glared at him when she'd been dancing with that guy had made it clear she wasn't happy with him. But for the life of him, he couldn't figure out what had happened. Not even her roommate had known.

To make matters worse, Darcy had refused to give him Sophia's name and number. Five years wasted wondering what was going through her head and not being able to move past the feelings he'd already developed for her.

Yes. He was definitely a little crazy.

"Anyway, you might want to count yourself lucky."

"How's that?" Cameron said.

"You know that if you give up now, you don't have to worry about her breaking your heart."

It was definitely too late for that. "You sure you don't know why she doesn't do second dates?"

Her brother tilted his head thoughtfully. "I don't honestly know. Ten years ago, my brother was left at the altar by his fiancée. She cheated on him. I think that hit Sophia harder than she wanted to admit. But five years ago, that's when she stopped entertaining second dates. She doesn't talk about what happened. She just insisted that she wasn't interested in settling down, and no one could convince her otherwise."

Cameron's stomach lurched. Five years ago was when they'd met. Could her reasons for avoiding commitment have something to do with their interaction? That didn't make sense. He hadn't done anything wrong.

He dragged his hand down his face. Now he definitely had to get to the bottom of what was going on. If he didn't, it would eat at him until he was a shell of who he was.

Sophia's brother chuckled again. "It's too late, isn't it?"

Cameron lifted his head and stared at him.

He jerked his chin toward his house. "You've already got a thing for her, huh?" There must have been a look of concern on his face because the man chuckled again. "Don't worry. I won't tell her. Won't tell Mateo, either. Somehow, I don't think he'd like that much. He's *really* protective."

"And you're not?"

Shrugging, he gave Cameron a smirk. "Let's just say that I think Sophia would be a lot easier to deal with if she found someone. She can be a real pain in the you know what."

Cameron smiled despite himself.

Shoving his hand outward, the guy's grin widened. "I'm Roman."

"Cameron."

"I know," he said simply. He turned to leave but then stopped and faced Cameron again. "If you know what's good for you, you'd walk away." He paused for a moment. "Then again, you might be just the thing to break her out of the prison she's put herself in."

Cameron watched him go, then shook his head with disbelief. That was weird.

7

———

Sophia

"**I**'ve got a babysitter, and that means that we're going out."

Sophia smiled as she glanced over at Emma—also known as Emily. The country music star had really slowed down since she'd had her first child. She still did a handful of shows across the country, but for the most part, she preferred to stay home with her family.

And who wouldn't when she had managed to find the perfect guy? Caleb Keagan had swept her off her feet, and she had been willing to change her whole life just for him.

She still looked like a star even after becoming a mom.

"What do you say? Girls' night?" she pleaded with Sophia, her bright blue eyes sparkling with excitement. "Caleb says we haven't gone dancing in ages, and he wants to take us to Shane's country club."

Sophia chewed on her lower lip. It had been forever

since she'd gone out with Emma. The handful of dates she'd gone on since they'd met had also been few and far between. And since Cameron came crashing back into her life? She'd only gone on one date, officially. Unofficially? She'd gone out to the country club to escape from the suffocating knowledge that Cameron was living on her family's property.

For some reason, she couldn't bring herself to actually go on a date.

"A girls' night sounds nice." Maybe she'd be able to forget about the tall, handsome man who had managed to steal her heart five years ago. The man she'd never really gotten over.

"Perfect! We'll pick you up. Seven sound good?"

Sophia nodded. She brought her drink to her lips and took a sip. It was a beautiful day, and it was a nice surprise when Emma dropped in to say hello. Caleb had wanted to speak to Mateo about something, so the two ladies had opted to get some lemonade and relax on the porch.

Emma let out a whistle. Her voice dropped to a whisper, and she nudged Sophia. "Are all of the guys your brother hired that good-looking? I mean, he's nothing like Caleb, but geez. You should definitely ask him out."

Sophia let her focus shift in the direction that Emma had motioned with her eyes, and her stomach dipped. Of course, she would say something like that about Cameron. Sophia scowled.

Emma laughed at her reaction. "He already get on your blacklist?"

"You could say that," Sophia muttered.

Her friend's eyes widened. "That sounds like a story I want to hear."

"It's not that interesting, really. He's just a flirt and a tease."

"Sounds like someone else I know."

Sophia gasped and dug her elbow into her friend's side. "How dare you?"

Emma shrugged. "All I'm saying is that you don't exactly go after one guy for long."

"Yeah, because we can't all be lucky enough to snag a Keagan."

Emma laughed. After a little while, she went quiet. "Well, if he's not an option, then who is? We need to find you a man."

Sophia rolled her eyes. "I don't need a man or anyone else. I have my family and my job. I'm perfectly happy."

The look her friend gave her made it clear she didn't agree, but at least she wasn't going to argue with Sophia about her opinion.

Movement from across the yard stopped her even if she had wanted to say something to that effect. Caleb and Mateo stopped to speak to Cameron for a moment, and then they resumed their walk toward the house. Caleb gestured toward Emma, and she got to her feet. "I'll see you tonight."

Sophia nodded. "See you then."

"Wow, you look *good*." Emma's compliment warmed Sophia's heart. "Caleb is going to have to fight guys off you with a bat."

"Unfortunately, I didn't bring it with me tonight, Sophia. So you're on your own." Caleb chuckled as he shut the truck door.

Sophia laughed with him. "Don't worry. I can handle myself." The country club was already in full swing. And yet all Sophia could think about was the last time she'd *really* enjoyed going dancing. She'd come here since meeting Cameron at the conference five years ago, but nothing had compared to that night she'd been in his arms.

She shook her head to clear it of the memories. The pain that came with those memories had become more potent ever since Cameron had shown up. And with that pain came additional memories of the first man who had ever betrayed her.

Closing her eyes briefly, she shoved those depressing thoughts deep into her soul where they wouldn't be capable of bothering her tonight.

She was here to have fun with her friends, and she refused to let her past stop her from doing so.

They entered the country club, the upbeat music making it easier to let her past fall away. Almost immediately, Caleb dragged Emma to the dance floor. Sophia waved at her, laughing at the squeal that escaped Emma's lips.

Once upon a time, Sophia had wanted to find that kind of love. But now she knew better. It was getting harder and harder to find someone who was so devoted that they would never leave the person they loved. Cheating and divorce rates only continued to grow higher. The fact that two members of her family had been affected by the former proved it.

Rather than jumping right into the fray and dancing with a stranger, Sophia moved to get a drink. She needed something fruity and bubbly—something to help her relax. She didn't want to blame Cameron's presence on the ranch for the tension in her muscles, but part of her knew that was exactly what had happened. He was everywhere. His eyes would remain trained on her whenever she entered his vicinity. Needless to say, she had been on edge, and it was all because some small part of her still had feelings for him.

That was crazy, right?

Yes, definitely crazy.

She got to the bar and placed her order. In no time at all, her defenses softened. She moved to the dance floor but didn't see Emma or Caleb anywhere. With a shrug of her shoulders, she let loose to the upbeat sound of the music playing. This place was tame when it came to dancing. It wasn't anything like the bar where she'd danced with Cameron five years ago. Shane did everything he could to make this place feel safe. Everything from the refreshments offered to the music was carefully curated. The lighting even made people feel safe to let loose.

While his country club was nothing like the bars and clubs where the younger population enjoyed mingling, it definitely wasn't your typical country club either. This place was a catchall that emulated the town of Copper Creek to a tee.

Sophia had only eaten once at the fancy restaurant that was part of this place. It was too highbrow for her liking. The ballroom was where it was at. Sophia could spend every weekend here just to get her social fix.

A woodsy, masculine scent enveloped her from behind, and she sensed she'd drawn a dance partner to her. A smile pulled at her lips, and she turned to find a cowboy with a smirk that matched her own. His moves were decent, but it was his charisma that intrigued her. He practically exuded confidence.

Cameron has something similar.

The flicker of a thought came out of left field, and Sophia's smile faltered. She wasn't supposed to be thinking about Cameron. He wasn't at the country club, and he wasn't going to get her attention anymore—bad or good. Once his contract was over, he'd move on and prove that she was right to keep him at arm's length.

The music slowed, and before Sophia could slip away from her dance partner, he slipped an arm around her waist and pulled her close. His right hand captured her left, and he led them both into a sultry sway.

"You're beautiful, but I'm guessing you already know that," he said. His voice was gravelly and low. Its husky timber immediately made her think about Cameron again.

Ugh! Why couldn't she get him out of her head? He was everywhere. It wasn't fair.

Sophia closed her eyes to shut out Cameron's face from her thoughts. He wasn't allowed to make her feel this way.

"You okay?" the stranger murmured near her ear.

She gasped, and her eyes opened. His dark brows were pulled together, though his eyes were bright with interest. Sophia nodded with a laugh. "Just a little dizzy. Maybe I should get some water—"

His hold on her tightened. Or was she imagining that? He offered her a knowing smile. "It's okay, beautiful. I can hold us both up."

"She said she wants a drink of water."

That voice. It was the one she heard in every single one of her dreams. It was the one that sent chills racing down her spine. That voice was the voice of an angel, and she knew before she turned around who would be behind her.

"If she wants to go, she can go," her stranger said to Cameron over her shoulder before looking down at her.

Before she had a chance to respond, Cameron's hand grasped the one she had resting on the stranger's shoulder. In a move that was as exhilarating as it was terrifying, he spun her away from her dance partner. He kept ahold of her hand with one of his own while placing the other on the small of her back.

Sophia glanced over her shoulder at the cowboy she'd left on the dance floor, her head still spinning. Then her eyes narrowed as she gave Cameron a disgruntled look. "What are you doing? I was dancing with him."

"And he wasn't listening to you."

"You don't know that—"

"I know more than you realize." Cameron jerked his chin toward the cowboy, who had already managed to find a replacement to dance with. "That guy is trouble."

She scoffed. "And you know this how?"

"Call it a gut instinct."

Sophia tugged at the hand he held, but he didn't release her until they made it to the counter, where he ordered her a bottle of water. She had the hardest time remaining mad at him for his intrusion as she leaned against the counter and peered up at him.

Cameron's eyes remained locked on her as she lifted the bottle to her lips. He actually looked concerned. Either it was that drink she'd had or his proximity, but she found herself smiling at him from beneath her lashes.

"Thank you," she murmured.

"For saving you from that guy?"

Sophia rolled her eyes and lifted the water.

He nodded, and then his focus shifted to the room. "You should be more careful."

"*Please*," she drawled. "You realize that this town isn't exactly a crime capitol, right? I'm perfectly safe."

"That doesn't mean anything," Cameron said. "Crime can happen in small towns, too. Your town is growing. People are moving here."

"So what does that make you? Are you a criminal I should be worried about?"

With an expression that was far too serious, Cameron shook his head. "I would never hurt you."

She arched a brow, tempted to tell him it was too late for that. But she shrugged that thought off. "Sorry, I'm not taking applications for a knight in shining armor. You're gonna have to go elsewhere."

That got him smiling, and geez it made her stomach flip like it had jumped off a plane without a parachute. He leaned in close to her, and his breath fanned her face as he said in a husky voice, "I'm well aware you don't need saving. But maybe you'd consider a partner in crime."

She laughed. She couldn't remember the last time she'd laughed like that.

And the grin he gave her after he heard that laugh? There went her stomach again.

"Does that mean you'll consider it?" His words were more like a growl than anything else.

She tilted her head to consider him, her lower lip protruding. Then she pressed her fingers against his chest until he stumbled back a step. "Sorry, bud. I work alone." She grinned at his dumbfounded expression as she dragged her fingertips down his chest and headed off in the direction that she'd just seen Emma go.

8

———

Cameron

Cameron turned to watch Sophia go.

That interaction hadn't been bad. Not at all.

She'd smiled at him. She'd flirted. That was the girl he'd fallen for in Texas through and through. His heart yearned to follow her to her friend and pull her into a dance for himself. She was the light, and he was an unsuspecting bug that couldn't keep his eyes from her.

The way she swayed her hips when she moved. The sound of her laugh.

That smile.

Oh boy. That woman was going to be the end of him.

In those few moments when they'd been standing beside each other, he'd forgotten all about the pain she'd caused him when she'd left him high and dry after agreeing to another date. He'd forgotten about the ache that had been dug into his chest when he realized she had refused to give him her name and a way to contact her.

In that moment? He'd gone back in time when anything was possible.

Cameron watched her from his position against the wall. His arms were folded, and he had lifted a boot to rest it against the wall at his back. From this distance, he could observe her and pretend that they had something more.

Eventually, he'd wear her down. He'd make her believe they were good for each other—just as soon as he figured out why she was pushing him away. There had to be a reason. No, he didn't know her as well as he wanted to, but he knew in his gut that she wasn't the type of person who would do something so heartless.

She glanced in his direction and their eyes locked for a few moments. She smiled before turning back to her friend. At one point that friend shot a peek at him, too. Then Sophia laughed at what her friend said.

They were talking about him, and he didn't mind at all.

Cameron winked at her when he caught her stare. She rolled her eyes, and the thrill of the chase returned. She wasn't going to be able to ignore him for long. She'd come back. There was a pull they had to each other. It tethered them together like nothing he'd ever experienced before. She belonged to him, and he belonged to her.

Now that he'd found her, he wasn't going anywhere. Whatever it took, he would get them back on track.

"Hey, cutie. I haven't seen you here before," a feminine voice purred at him. He didn't have to look at the woman to know that she was a little shorter than he was. "You here alone?" There was a pout to her voice and for a brief second, his focus darted to her. She was blonde and had full lips. She had a more slender frame than Sophia did, and her eyes were a pretty shade of blue, but she was no Sophia.

He grasped her hand and pulled it away from his shirt. "I'm not here alone."

Her eyes flickered with desire. "Really, well... would you like some company?"

Cameron's attention shifted to where he'd last seen Sophia, but she wasn't there. He straightened and scanned the room as he released the girl's hand. "No thanks. There's actually someone else..."

She reached for him again, but this time he shoved off the wall and moved away.

"Thanks, but I'm not interested." He offered her an apologetic smile before moving away from her and searching the room. Where had Sophia gone? He caught sight of her friend on the dance floor with a guy. But no Sophia. She might have gone outside for some air. Or she might be dancing. She could have gone to the bathroom.

A wash of anxiety splashed over him as he thought back to the guy who was clearly ignoring her request when she'd said she wanted water. Sure, the guy might have been harmless, but he might have had ulterior motives, too. There was no telling what kind of man he was.

The way Sophia drew people in with her smile meant she could be welcoming all sorts of miscreants. He had this gut-wrenching feeling that she needed protection despite what she'd said earlier—though he would never have said so himself. He couldn't afford to scare her off or push her away.

Moving through the crowds of people who were now swarming onto the dance floor for an upbeat country song, Cameron's focus continued to dart from one side of the large space to the other.

The people were now dancing in lines and moving as one. Someone bumped into him, nearly knocking him off balance. He couldn't see Sophia in the waves of people. That didn't surprise him. She didn't seem like the type to enjoy a choreographed line dance.

There were only a few individuals on the edges of the room as they took a break from the physical requirements of the dance.

Still, no Sophia.

He frowned. While he could hang out right beside the bathrooms, he didn't think Sophia would appreciate finding him stalking her like that—even if he'd made the excuse that he wanted to ask her to dance next. They hadn't had a chance to dance yet, and that was the main reason he'd asked around.

Roman had mentioned his sister came here frequently, but the look on his face when he mentioned it made it clear he didn't approve of Cameron's interest. It was unclear if he disapproved because he wanted to protect Sophia or if he wanted to protect Cameron.

The song was nearing its end by the time Cameron moved to the door that opened out onto a balcony on the back side of the space.

He heard her voice before he saw her. Turning the corner, he froze. Sophia had both of her arms draped around the back of some guy's neck. She was staring up at him like he was a superhero. Cameron couldn't see the guy's face, but he could see the way Sophia looked at him, and it made his blood boil.

Watching the two of them was utter torture. He could remember what it felt like when she looked at him like that. It chased away the darkness and made him believe he could do anything. His fingers curled around, forming a fist as he heard the man's chuckle. There was no deciphering their words.

Sophia's eyes snagged on Cameron, and her smile widened before she turned her attention to the lucky cowboy who had his hands at her waist. She tilted her head in that flirtatious way that could snare any man with a heart.

As the cowboy lowered his face toward Sophia, her eyes shifted to Cameron. It was brief and might have been hard to see for anyone who didn't know Sophia well, but she attempted to pull back from the guy. The smile on her face looked strained, like she was regretting the position she was in. Her gaze shifted to Cameron once more, and that was all it took for him to launch forward. He laid a heavy hand on the cowboy's shoulder and jerked him backward.

"Cameron!" Sophia gasped. "What are you—"

"Hey, man—" the cowboy said.

Cameron ignored them both as he grasped Sophia's hand in his own and pulled her away from the man who had nearly kissed her. "Who was that?" he ground out.

She tugged on his hold of her, but he refused to release her. Instead, he pulled her through the crowd. They passed by her friends, who called out her name, but he didn't stop for them.

"*Cameron*," her voice was indignant and fueled with irritation. "What are you doing?"

"That guy," he huffed as they burst through the front door. "Who was he?"

"No one."

He pulled her to a sudden stop, and his eyes narrowed on her. "That guy doesn't mean anything to you, and you were just going to... *what*? Let him kiss you?" He could hear the fury in his voice, the betrayal too, but he didn't care—especially when he noted the flicker of regret in her gaze. But even that reaction quickly faded.

She yanked her hand from his grasp. "It's none of your business who I kiss or don't kiss. You're not my boyfriend."

"Neither is he."

"Exactly. And I'm allowed to kiss whomever I want to—"

He pointed at the truck. "Get in."

Her eyes darted to the side, having just realized that he'd stopped at his vehicle. "What?"

"Get in the truck, Sophia. I'm taking you home."

She barked out a laugh. "You can't be serious. I didn't come here with you."

"I'm aware. But I'm taking you home."

She folded her arms and defiance flickered in her eyes. "No."

He arched a brow. If he really wanted to, he could throw her in that truck himself, but he would rather she got in all by herself. Taking a deep, calming breath, he lowered his voice so it resembled less of a growl and more like a plea. "Get in the truck, Sophia."

That defiant streak faltered. "Why?"

Cameron couldn't tell her that he had been blinded by jealousy and that was the only reason he wanted to remove her from this place—that there were far too many red-blooded males to make him comfortable. He couldn't tell her that he was in love with her and had been for five years. She'd laugh in his face. So he went with the only reason that might make a difference.

"You're being reckless."

"Reckless?" she said, stamping a foot. "I'm *not* reckless."

"I've been watching you tonight. You're definitely not paying attention."

She huffed this time, her voice surprised and maybe a little disgusted. "You've been spying on me?"

Cameron opened the door and motioned for her to get in, but she shook her head. He took a step toward her so she would focus on him. "What would your brother say if I told him about the guy who wouldn't listen to you? Or that other guy? You didn't want him to kiss you, did you?"

She glared at him, but she didn't deny what he said. Sophia didn't even try to move away from him.

He inched his face closer to hers, his voice lowered to that husky tone she remembered from before. "But what about me? Would you pull away if I wanted to steal a kiss from you? Would you fight me off if I claimed your mouth for my own?"

Her lips parted, but she didn't utter a word.

Still, he moved a little closer. "Because I don't think you would. Do you know why, Red?"

"Why?" she whispered.

Before he could tell her, a couple approached, the girl laughing aloud at something her date had said. Sophia took a step backward. She looked at the couple, then shifted her attention to him. The glare returned, and she pushed past him to climb into the passenger seat. Without a word, she pulled on her seatbelt and faced forward.

He watched her for a moment, and then he shut the door.

9

Sophia

Sophia had never been this on edge before. The second Cameron climbed behind the steering wheel, she couldn't keep still. His words echoed in her head, bouncing around until it made her dizzy. She couldn't bring herself to look in his direction because he'd been right. He'd hit the metaphorical nail on the head with everything.

She had been uncomfortable with the two men. The first guy hadn't been too bad, but the relief she'd felt over Cameron intervening had been palpable.

The second guy was a stupid mistake. Emma had nearly convinced her to go over to Cameron and ask him to dance when she'd caught sight of him with that blonde Barbie. The only way to describe the emotions that churned inside her at witnessing the two of them together had been hot, fiery rage. It brought her back to the night she'd caught him with that girl outside of his hotel room.

Both had been blondes. Both had been the stereotypical women she saw in every magazine. It made her feel sick to her stomach, and she'd wanted to make Cameron hurt for it. So, she'd found the first guy she could and flirted with him mercilessly.

That woman had her hands all over Cameron, and while Sophia had no claim to him, she couldn't deny the ache that reared its ugly head when she saw him with someone else.

The fury was so opposite of the longing she had for that man, and it only served to add to her confusion. How could she want someone who would only toy with her? It didn't make sense.

She let her eyes drift toward Cameron, noting how hard he was gripping the steering wheel. He wasn't thrilled to be in here with her. But she didn't know why. If he was so upset with her, why did he even bother taking her home?

"Message your friends," he said.

Startled, she glanced at his face. His jaw was tight, and his eyes remained locked on the road.

Cameron continued, "Tell them you caught a ride home. They'll be worried about you."

She nodded numbly and pulled her phone from her back pocket. Once she had sent off the message and told Emma she would fill her in later, she put the phone into her lap and turned her attention to the window.

Part of her wanted to thank him for what he'd done for her. When he'd stepped in, he had helped her even if she didn't want to admit it to herself—or him. But she couldn't. She would never show him her weaknesses because that was what these feelings were. She was weak. What kind of person caught feelings for a guy who was unattainable? And she would know because she was the female equivalent of unattainability.

The irony of this situation wasn't lost on her. The universe was laughing at her, watching her fall for a guy who would never want her back—not in the way she'd need him to.

She stared out the window, unseeing as she relived the evening and the other interactions she'd had with Cameron. When they arrived at her home, she lurched from the truck and practically ran toward the house. The last thing she wanted was for Cameron to walk her to her door. Sophia could do without the temptation of kissing him.

Because whether she liked it or not, he'd been right about that, too. If he'd wanted to steal a kiss, she would have let him and loved every second of it.

THE FOLLOWING days were filled with as much tension as the ones leading up to that night at the country club. Sophia couldn't forget the way Cameron had looked at her when that guy had nearly kissed her. Whenever she closed her eyes, all she saw was the look in his eyes when Cameron whispered what would happen if he were to be the one kissing her.

The simple act of remembering that moment was enough to give her goosebumps, and it was really starting to get old.

When she entered the barn that morning, Cameron tossed her a saddle bag. "We're going for a ride."

She lifted a brow. "I beg your pardon? I have work to—"

"Mateo and Daniel signed off on it. We're taking a couple

dogs with us. Trained ones who haven't been out in a couple days. Everyone's a little antsy." He gave her a pointed look, and her stomach had once again turned into an acrobat. She had definitely grown antsy. Her body practically buzzed to be touched by him.

Sophia put her hands on her hips. His focus dipped to her waist, and he turned toward the two horses that had already been saddled. The light from the sun was only just filling the sky. In about thirty minutes, it would be rising over the mountains toward the east.

He wasn't trying to take her to see a sunrise, was he? No. He wouldn't go to the trouble. He'd said himself, this was something Mateo wanted. She frowned as she headed toward the horse and climbed into the saddle.

"They need some exercise, but I also want to see how they handle the terrain. If they have any weak muscles, then I'll be able to take note and get the vet to come do a physical. We want these girls in top physical condition before we get them ready for breeding." Cameron said all of this without looking at her directly. He focused on securing his own pack and ensuring that the saddle was how he wanted it to be.

Then in one quick movement, he was situated in the saddle, the Stetson on his head giving him a rugged cowboy look. He led the way out of the barn, and at that moment, Mateo materialized with two of his favorite ranch dogs. He crouched down and scratched each of them with affection, then jerked his chin toward Cameron and Sophia. "Behave."

Cameron smirked, and Sophia snickered before she whistled for the dogs to follow. They loped beside her as she followed Cameron out to the nearest trail. Her eyes remained locked on the back of Cameron's head. There was so much that had been left unspoken. Since that night,

Cameron hadn't said a word to her that wasn't related to the animals. Maybe he was embarrassed. Or he could have regret for how he'd treated her.

Sophia sighed. She didn't like the person she'd become around him. Under normal circumstances, she didn't avoid the men in her life. To be fair, those men were all very aware that she didn't do relationships, so there wasn't the implication that anything would come after their interaction.

She urged her horse forward so she could ride beside him. Cameron glanced at her, his face unreadable. Of course. Cameron was a master at hiding how he felt. The closest he'd gotten to showing her his feelings was at the country club. He'd almost appeared worried for her. She knew better than to believe he was jealous.

Even if things felt weird between them, she wasn't going to let him see that. Sophia straightened her shoulders and flashed him a smile. "So, do you like it here? In Copper Creek?"

Cameron offered a smile back, and it almost looked genuine. He nodded. "It's nice. A lot different than Texas."

She barked out a laugh. "Definitely. Just wait until winter comes."

He smirked. "Can't wait."

Sophia tilted her head, eyeing him for a moment. "Did you grow up in Texas?"

Cameron nodded. "I did."

"I bet the change in weather up here is a lot different than you're used to."

"I've been all over. I'm probably more used to this sort of thing than you realize."

"Really?" Her brows lifted. "Do you really travel that much for work?"

Cameron's body language relaxed, and he nodded. "I didn't used to travel, but that changed a couple years ago."

"What place is your favorite?"

He glanced at her before he rolled his shoulders and opened his mouth. But then he closed his mouth and rubbed a hand down his face. "Tell me something, Red. In Texas—"

Why did he have to go there? She shook her head. "I don't live in the past, Cameron. I've moved on from Texas." *Lies.* "I'd rather live my life to the fullest." She prayed he couldn't hear the way her voice shook. The last thing she needed was for him to point out that he could tell she was lying through her teeth.

He frowned, and his jaw tightened. Clearly, he didn't like her response.

The friendly conversation shut down just like that. She didn't want to talk about Texas, and he did. Well, tough luck for him. She wasn't going to linger on one of the more depressing moments of her life.

They entered a clearing where a couple cowboys hovered around something on the ground. The dogs at her side bolted, and she shot a concerned look to Cameron before she knocked her boots to her horse's side.

A calf lay on the ground, apparently mauled by an animal.

Sophia gasped and jumped down from her horse. She moved up to Mark's side. She grabbed his forearm and said, "What do you think happened?"

"Wolves." Mark spat. He raked a hand through his hair, then returned his hat there. "We'll have to tell Mateo about it. Sounds like the ranch on the western side of the property has had a few sightings."

Sophia frowned. This neighboring pasture was on the outskirts of their property. If they were lucky, they wouldn't get any unwanted visitors. She stared down at the calf with a heavy heart. "Poor thing."

Mark nodded. Unfortunately, this was the way of life on a ranch. He glanced at her, and a smile broke across his face. "Hey, on a better note, I've been meaning to tell you something." He leaned in close, his voice dropping to a whisper. His hand reached for her upper arm as he did. "I'm proposing to Tracy this weekend."

She reared back and grinned at him before she threw her arms around his neck and gave him a tight hug. "I knew it." When she pulled back, she could feel the hot stare of the man who was still seated in his saddle. It bore into her and nearly set her insides on fire. When she glanced at him, she noted the anger marring the handsome lines of his face. What on earth was wrong with him?

Her eyes narrowed, and she shook her head in exasperation. Mark glanced over at him after noting her attention. He lifted a brow. "He seems... nice."

"Yeah," she said. "Real nice." Then she smiled at Mark again. "Tell me how it goes. I want details."

Mark nodded. "Of course."

When she was back on her horse, she wasn't surprised that the remainder of the ride continued in silence. Cameron was in a sour mood, and there was nothing she could do about it. Nor did she care.

"WHAT DO YOU MEAN, you know him?" Emma said into the speaker.

Sophia stared at the ceiling, her phone pressed to her ear. Emma had finally convinced her to spill the truth about Cameron after the ridiculous night that had been the country club outing. "I met him five years ago when I went to a conference in Texas."

"And?" Emma urged. "What happened?"

Sophia pressed her finger and thumb into her closed eyes. "Nothing happened. We flirted. He wore me down, and I told him I'd go on a date with him. Then another." She groaned, detailing what had happened after that. The whole thing was still just as heartbreaking.

Emma let out a whistle. "Okay, now it totally makes sense."

"What makes sense?" Sophia asked. "The fact that he can still make me jealous?"

"Well, to be fair, he looked pretty jealous, too."

Sophia snorted. "No. He's just... I don't know... controlling."

"You sure about that?"

"That's the only thing that makes sense. If he was jealous, then he wouldn't have let that girl put her hands all over him. And that girl in Texas? It's the same thing. He's got the attention of any girl he wants. He doesn't have to be jealous about me being with guys."

Emma was quiet for a moment. "I don't know, Soph. Maybe you should corner him and demand he explain himself. He was supposed to go on a date with you, and you said yourself that he showed up at the club you were at. Maybe there's more to this story."

"There isn't. Thanks for trying to make me feel better, but honestly, I think it would be better if I forget about him and move on. I don't need this kind of drama. You should have seen the way he was glaring at me today. It was like I'm not allowed to be friends with a guy because I didn't fall to his whims or something."

"Sounds like jealousy to me."

Sophia rolled her eyes. She knew jealousy. That wasn't jealousy.

"You know what they say. If you want to move on, then the best thing to do is clear the air. So talk to him."

"Maybe," Sophia muttered noncommittally. She definitely wasn't going to do that. She didn't need to see the triumph on his face when he realized that she had been hurt by his philandering ways.

10

———

Cameron

*L*ungs burning, Cameron lurched to a stop and hunched over as he drew in oxygen with gulps of air. He rose upward with a hand on his hip as he wiped the sweat from his brow. He used to run a lot when he was in high school. When he was younger, it was for the endorphins he gained from the exercise.

Now, it was to rid himself of the emotions that threatened to take away his control. The way Sophia let down her walls around the men who worked for her brother was eating at him. Those smiles she gave them weren't anything like the guarded ones she offered him, and it was driving him crazy.

Yesterday, she'd hugged that cowboy—Mark was his name—and she'd laughed with him for a few minutes before she'd finally returned to their ride. He'd refused to bring it up because he knew it would only start a fight. He didn't want to admit that the way she treated him was eating at him. If she knew just how frustrated he was, she'd definitely use it against him.

The optimistic side of him wanted to believe that she was opening up to him, but after seeing her interaction with Mark, he knew that was laughable. Sophia was a different person around him, and he wasn't getting any closer to making her see him as anything other than her enemy.

Her voice drew his attention, and his head whipped around as he watched her climb out of a truck and head for the house. There was a man closing the passenger door that she'd just vacated. He waved at her, then climbed back in the truck to drive away.

Cameron narrowed his eyes at the cowboy. The guy didn't work for Mateo, and he wasn't the same guy who had been dancing with Sophia's friend at the country club.

The poisonous jealousy that urged him to go after Sophia and demand to know who she'd been with threatened to overtake his self-control. She didn't belong to him, and he wasn't going to push her away more than he already had.

He turned on his heel and nearly collided with a young woman. She gasped and her lashes fluttered. Her deep blue eyes darted from him to Sophia and back, then a slow smile touched her lips. She was Sophia's sister, and according to the ramblings of the other cowboys, she was the beauty of the three. But not to Cameron. No one was more striking than Sophia. He hadn't spoken to this sister, even after being here for several weeks, and he couldn't recall her name.

Her arms folded across her chest, and she tilted her head. "You have something for Sophia, don't you?"

Cameron frowned. If she'd noticed and Roman had

noticed, then it was only a matter of time before Mateo figured it out. According to Roman, that was something he needed to avoid. Cameron shoved his hands into his pockets and shrugged. "I don't know what you're talking about."

She snorted. "I've seen the way you look at her. It's pretty obvious."

Man. How could everybody tell how he felt?

"Whatever you think you've seen, I can assure you—"

"Whatever, dude. I don't care. Honestly, it's probably a good thing."

"It is?"

She nodded. "You're clearly a little obsessed with her."

He stiffened. That didn't sound *good* at all.

This time, she laughed. "Relax, dude. After what she's dealt with, I think the only guy she would trust is someone who clearly only has eyes for her."

There was so much to unload with that statement. He moved closer to Sophia's sister. "What has she been through?"

At that point, she seemed to have realized that she had said something wrong. Her cheeks blushed, and she glanced at the house with worry before she brought her gaze back to him. "I'm not supposed to know about it."

"What happened?" he said gently. "I'm really trying to figure out what's going on—why she seems to hate me so much."

She worried her lower lip. "I probably shouldn't say anything."

His hand reached to touch her arm before she thought to escape. "Please," he whispered. "I do care about her. You caught me. But I can't get close to her if she won't open up to me, and if there's a way for me to help her, then I want to know how."

Sophia's sister glanced to the house once more, then nodded. "Fine. All I know is she was really close with her high school sweetheart. They were seeing each other for the longest time. I thought they were going to get married. I think Sophia thought so, too. But then within days of my brother's fiancée leaving him at the altar, Sophia's boyfriend stopped hanging around. Sophia sorta withdrew. She didn't act like herself. One of my friends heard rumors that her boyfriend was cheating on Sophia with like three other girls. Well... he was technically cheating on all of them. They just didn't know because they went to different schools. I don't know how Sophia figured it out. But..." She shrugged her shoulders.

Cameron hadn't realized his hands were balled into fists until the bite of his nails brought his attention to it. No wonder she didn't go on second dates. She didn't trust that men would stay faithful. She flirted with everyone and didn't get attached.

Sophia had said she didn't trust easily. It was one of her reasons for turning him down. But this didn't answer the burning question as to why she'd agreed to a second date, only to leave him hanging.

"You okay?"

The girl's soft voice yanked him to the present and he stared down at her with a grim expression. "Yeah. Fine. Thanks."

She nodded, then turned to head past him, but he stopped her.

"Sorry, I didn't catch your name."

Turning, she flashed him a small smile. "Isabelle."

He watched her hurry toward the house and breathed out a sigh as he turned in the direction of the wranglers' cabin. After that interaction, he could use another run, but it was getting late. He'd have to wait until tomorrow.

CAMERON RISKED another glance at Sophia. She didn't look pleased with him, and why would she be? The last time they'd spent time together, he'd glowered at her until she left in a huff. He really needed to work on that. He wasn't going to draw her in if he was constantly angry. Sophia was the light, and she drew every unsuspecting man to it, including himself.

He breathed out a sigh and forced his expression to relax. She was allowed to have a life here. There would always be competition until he finally won her over. With that in mind, he leaned against the stall door beside him and flashed her a smile.

She glanced up at him just in time for the door to creak and give beneath his weight. It hadn't been latched, and he stumbled into the empty stall with a crash.

Sophia snickered. It was Friday, and what he really wanted to do was ask her out. To get her to open up. He scrambled out of the stall and folded his arms as he leaned against a pole instead.

"You think that's funny, huh?" He glanced up at her with s small smile on his face. "I was thinking—"

She eyed him momentarily, then held up her hand. "Save it, Cameron. We work together because we *have* to. That's it. Let's not pretend that we're anything but adversaries."

"*Adversaries*—"

"Sophia! Emma is here." Isabelle's face materialized at the doorway to the barn.

"Tell her I'll be right there. I just have to jump in the shower."

Isabelle nodded, and Sophia returned the brush she had in her hand to the shelf. She gave him a parting look, then headed out before he could get another word in edgewise.

It would draw too much unwanted attention for him to chase after her, calling her name. Though there was a part of him that was willing to do just that if he didn't think Sophia would chew him out over it.

If Emma had shown up to go out with her, then the two of them were likely going to that country club. Already, his jealousy was rearing its ugly head. He couldn't stand the thought of her in anyone else's arms but his own. Why couldn't they get on the same page?

Okay, he knew why. And it had a lot to do with the unanswered questions of their past.

He scowled after her as a thought formulated in his mind. There was only one way to get past that hurdle. He'd need to confront her about it.

Cameron lay in wait for Sophia to return. It was nearing midnight, and he felt like his heart was trying to claw itself right out of his chest. It thundered with each passing hour, and he wondered how hard it would be to track her down in this small town if she *wasn't* at that club.

There was already a dirt trail getting embedded into the grass near the side of her house as he continued to pace where he could see her when she returned. His hair had become mussed and untamed. He probably looked like a wild creature, and maybe he was beginning to realize that he shouldn't be waiting to pounce on Sophia like he currently was.

As that pinprick of logic broke through the clouds of frustration that hovered around him, he made a move to head back to his room in the wranglers' cabin, but that plan was thwarted when a truck pulled up to the house and headlights locked him in place.

Cameron couldn't see the faces of the individuals in the truck from where he stood. All he knew was that this wasn't the same vehicle that Sophia had left in. His hands curled tightly at his sides when a stranger stepped from the driver's side and gave him a wary look.

The cowboy wasn't much taller than Sophia, which had him shorter than Cameron's six-foot frame. He hurried around the truck to open the door for Sophia, and she stepped into Cameron's line of sight. She frowned at Cameron before flashing this cowboy a smile and giving him a hug. Then she said something to him and nodded. The cowboy stayed by his truck, watching her head toward the front entrance of her home. Cameron stepped forward.

"Sophia—"

"What do you think you're doing?" she hissed.

"We need to talk."

She scoffed like she had no intention of doing any such thing, but then she waved the man off. "It's fine, Tad. He's a friend."

Cameron watched the guy move back to the driver's side. He hesitated before climbing behind the wheel, but eventually he pulled away.

"What is this about?" she said, drawing his attention to her again. "It's late, and I—"

"Why do you hate me so much?" The words tumbled from his lips, and he couldn't take them back. All he could do was wait for her answer.

11

———

Sophia

"What?" Sophia blurted. Heat rose to her face, and she was grateful that he wouldn't be able to see the way he affected her. "Don't be ridiculous." She moved to get past him, but he stepped in front of her means of escape. Maybe she should have accepted Tad's offer to walk her to her door. What had she been thinking when she told him Cameron was harmless? The way he got her heart racing should have been all the proof she needed that he definitely wasn't that.

Cameron's eyes flashed with a myriad of emotions. The two that she was able to take note of were the anger and the pain. She knew those emotions well. They'd been good friends of hers since she'd been betrayed by her ex. "Don't lie to me, Sophia. You're not very good at it."

Her eyes widened, and her mouth fell open. "I beg your pardon?"

He stepped in closer, and his hands wrapped gently around her upper arms as he stared harder into her eyes. "You can't tell me that something isn't going on between us. You might think you're hiding it well, but you're wrong. *Dead wrong.*"

For a brief moment she wanted to tell him everything—how he'd hurt her when he'd made her feel like she was all he'd ever needed, only to be hooking up with other women. She wanted to fling it in his face that she knew *him* better than he knew her. She'd been around men like Cameron, and they weren't all Boy Scouts. But just reliving those memories had her heart tearing apart.

It was silly. Logically, she could admit that to herself. They'd barely known each other, and they hadn't exactly laid out any rules for seeing one another. What right did she have to be angry with him for keeping his options open?

But the romantic in her refused to acknowledge any of that. He'd pursued *her*. He'd made her feel special. When they'd been together, she'd allowed him to tear down her walls and she'd thought that maybe there had been a chance for her to find love again—to *trust* again.

She scowled and yanked out of his grasp as she bit back the tears that threatened to sting her eyes. "You don't know what you're talking about."

"Don't I?" he bit out. "You can't tell me that you didn't feel it. We had something good going on. There was a connection—"

"Get out of my way, Cameron. It's late, and I'm tired." She tried to block out the words he'd just said, tried to stitch up the emotional damage they were causing in her soul. Yes, they'd had a connection, but she wasn't the type of girl to go for a guy who didn't want to go all in with the girl he was chasing.

Cameron still blocked her path, and she had half a mind to scream bloody murder just so one of her brothers would come out and cart Cameron away for her. She scowled at him still, her eyes shooting daggers at him as best as they could. He scowled right back. Did he seriously not know what he'd done? Did he not see what kind of person he was? He lifted a hand to reach for her, but she jerked out of his grasp. His mouth set into a hard line before he heaved a sigh. "Do you know how frustrating it is to see the person you're interested in come home with a different guy every weekend?"

Her jaw dropped. The hypocrisy of it all! "That's rich, coming from you."

"What?" he said, his brows furrowed.

She poked him hard in the chest as she prowled closer to him this time. She emphasized each word with the touch of her finger. "Don't. Dish. It. Out. If. You. Can't. Take. It."

In a split second, he captured her finger in his hand and pulled so she stumbled forward a step. "What are you talking about, Sophia?" he growled. "I'm not the one going out every weekend with people I barely know."

"Who says I don't know them?" Sophia's heated whisper faltered, and she prayed he didn't see what his proximity was doing to her. She could smell his clean, woodsy scent, and it floated to her on the breeze between them. If she wasn't careful, she was going to lose her head and end up having her heart broken all over again.

Cameron scoffed. "What did I say about lying to me?" When she didn't answer, he adjusted his hold on her so he was no longer holding her finger but both of her hands. His voice softened, and that pain he'd been hiding seeped into his words. "What happened five years ago, Red? It never added up. I deserve to know."

All the pain and suffering she'd experienced after letting her guard down came rushing to the surface, and she hated him for his ability to seek it out like a hound dog. Mingled with that pain was a distinct sense of anger that she couldn't shake. He deserved to hurt—a lot more than he was hurting right now.

"Fine," she said, tugging on her hands but unable to escape his clutches. "You want to know what happened? I'll tell you what happened." She finally freed herself and folded her arms tight across her chest. "You made such a show of chasing me—of making me feel like I was the very moon that hung in the sky. *Special*." Her voice cracked. "You made me feel like there was still a chance that I could find happiness with someone after all the heartache I'd experienced in the past. I didn't want to let you in. I knew it wouldn't be smart to open up to someone I barely knew, and surprise, surprise. I was right."

His scowl remained fixed on his face, not giving her any indication of what he was feeling, so she trudged onward.

"You finally convinced me to give you a chance, and what did you do? You squandered it."

"I did no such thing. You were the one who ran off with another date that night," he ground out.

"Really? And who was that girl at your hotel room door?"

He frowned, the anger fading fast as confusion replaced it. His eyes shifted to the side while he returned to his own memories.

She barked out a laugh. "Why am I not surprised that you can't even remember her? Tall. Leggy. Blonde." She spat the words like venom. "You two were talking, and she was laughing, then she got a goodbye kiss from you. How many women, exactly, did you chase that week, huh?" Sophia shook her head with another huff and took a step to the side to finally escape Cameron. He had the answers he had wanted, and she needed to escape him before the first tear fell.

His hand grasped her wrist, stopping her escape.

"Cameron," she snapped, "let go of me or I'll—"

"There wasn't anyone else," Cameron whispered.

She stilled at the pleading in his tone as she slowly lifted her eyes to meet his. There was a new sort of ache in them that halted her decision to bolt.

His hold on her tightened. "You have to believe me."

"Why should I?" she asked, hating the desperation in her voice. Why was she so willing to get reeled back into his clutches? He was a spider, and she was the fly. At this point it wouldn't take much for her to become trapped in his web, and she wasn't sure if she hated that idea all that much.

Cameron tugged her closer to him before securing her at her waist. Sophia's hands landed on his chest as she stared up at him. What was it about the way he looked at her that made her wish he actually had a reasonable explanation?

"You came to my room early, didn't you?" he rasped.

She blinked, heat flushing her cheeks in an intolerable way.

"That girl was drunk. She'd come to the wrong room."

Sophia blinked again, not daring to believe what he was saying as much as she wanted to.

Cameron shut his eyes briefly, then shook his head with a wry sort of chuckle. "She'd thrown herself at me without looking too closely. I think she thought she was kissing the guy who had told her to meet him at his room that night." He opened his eyes, pleading with her. "You have to believe me, Red. I have no idea who that woman was. I pushed her away as soon as she kissed me. I ended up helping her find that room, too."

Sophia's stomach dropped, and her heart raced at his words. As much as she didn't want to believe him or give him the benefit of the doubt, she couldn't deny that the story made sense. She hadn't stuck around after the kiss to see if he'd done what he'd said. A groan escaped her chest, and the blush she knew had taken root in her cheeks grew hotter.

Placing her head against his chest so he couldn't see her face, she muttered under her breath.

"Hey," Cameron's soft voice broke the silence, and he shifted back so he could tilt her chin up to meet her eyes.

She closed them and shook her head.

"Red," he murmured more firmly this time, causing her to finally look at him. "What's going on?"

An embarrassed laugh escaped her lips, and she shook her head. "I'm such an idiot."

One side of his mouth quirked upward, but he shook his head, too. Cameron traced the line of her jaw with his knuckle as his eyes took her in. "You're not an idiot, Red."

"You don't have to be nice. I was being an idiot. I was hotheaded, and I didn't stick around to find out what was really happening. I just..." She pulled back from him. There were a million reasons why she couldn't stand here and pretend that she wasn't broken. And she wasn't about to give him the reason she'd jumped so quickly to assuming he was the villain.

Cameron's hands remained at her waist even though

they weren't pressed together anymore. His eyes searched hers, and he tilted his head. "Does this mean you'll give me another chance?"

She cut him a wary look, tempted but knowing it would be a bad idea. She wasn't in the right headspace, even knowing the truth. This time she took a big enough step away from him to force him to release her. "I don't date, Cameron. You know that."

His brows creased. "Why? I told you what happened—"

Sophia placed a hand on his chest, the temptation to tell him everything hovering just below the surface. She forced a smile and shrugged, deciding it was best to keep everything to herself. "I'm just not interested in something long-term. Don't think I'm built for it."

"I don't believe that."

Her eyes grew wide at his husky tone. "What?"

"You heard me. If you want me to believe that you're not craving that sort of connection, you're going to have to do a lot better than some flippant excuse like that."

She glowered at him. "You might think you know me, but you have no idea." Sophia shoved past him, and just as she pushed the front door open, she heard him call out to her.

"I'm going to change your mind, Red."

Sophia didn't bother turning back at his words. She simply shut the door behind her and escaped into the safety of her home.

12

Cameron

hy didn't Sophia want Cameron to know that she'd been betrayed by her boyfriend? It didn't make sense.

Unless she blamed herself.

But that was ridiculous. She had to know that the jerk's choices were his own. Sophia was smarter than that.

It had been another week since that conversation had taken place. Sophia wasn't exactly avoiding him anymore, and if he were honest, he'd admit she was actually opening up to him now—in some ways, at least. Topics that were off-limits related to relationships and dating. When she even sensed that he might bring it up, she walked away.

While he didn't relish the fact that she opted to ignore what was right in front of her, it wasn't as bad as it had been when she'd straight-up avoided him. She'd let him in again. He just had to bide his time.

His hands roamed over the horse in front of him as he checked over her body. The animal was in perfect condition. Today he'd be putting her in a pasture with the stallion to gauge her receptiveness. The teasing process shouldn't take long, and since the male that Mateo had chosen would be breeding with three of the brood mares on this property, the horses were familiar enough with him.

Cameron felt her gaze on him before he even realized she was within his vicinity. He glanced up to find Sophia watching him from where she leaned in the barn doorway. Immediately she looked away and pushed her body from that position before turning and leaving his sight.

A smile tugged at his lips. This was also something that had happened frequently enough to make him believe that she wanted more. She hadn't taken back her statement regarding her stance on dating, but the way she watched him made it clear she might have jumped the gun on her decision.

It would be so much easier if she'd just let go and let him get close to her again.

He chuckled with a shake of his head.

Sophia returned shortly after, hands in her back pockets. "She ready to go to the pasture with our stallion?"

Cameron arched a brow, the smile toying at his lips. "Do you mean, is she ready to face her fate and give in to her carnal desires?"

A pretty flush sprinkled across Sophia's cheeks. "If you want to call it that."

"I think I do."

She shrugged and looked away. "Fine. That then. Is she ready?"

Cameron eyed her with a mischievous grin, not missing

the way she fought a smile. "She's primped and relaxed—the perfect condition to meet the love of her life."

Sophia rolled her eyes, and he chuckled. Together they walked the mare toward the pasture. Sophia was at his side, and her arm brushed against his on their way. It wouldn't have taken any effort whatsoever for him to capture her hand within his own at this point. The temptation ate at him, but he wouldn't do that. Not yet.

He couldn't deny the thrill that her proximity gave him. Now that he knew why she'd behaved the way she had five years ago, he was finding it harder to give her the space she thought she needed. And from the looks of it, she was struggling with the same thing.

Her shoulder bumped into his, and he gave her his most charming smile. "You know what I like about you?"

Sophia glanced at him, a smirk gracing her beautiful, full lips. She tapped her finger to her chin. "My dance moves."

He groaned with appreciation, making her laugh, which was exactly what he wanted her to do. Then he cocked his head to the side and eyed her again. "Your dance moves are something else, but no, that's not what I was thinking."

She was hanging on his every word. Based on the way she was leaning into him, waiting for him to tell her exactly what he found so fascinating about her, he was already celebrating. She might think that she wasn't ready for anything serious, but nothing could be further from the truth. "What were you thinking, then?"

Cameron pulled himself to a stop and turned to face her. He reached up and tucked a strand of hair behind her ear. He could tell her he loved her eyes, her lips, her smile, her laugh. He could tell her that he adored her tenacity and her unwillingness to crumble when things got hard. There were already a hundred things he could tell her that would make her begin to see he wasn't going to let her go as easily as she expected.

But he wouldn't. He needed to draw her in—to snare her in a way that made it difficult for her to consider leaving him at all. Her breath hitched at his touch, and he held back the urge he had to pull her in for a kiss. Instead, he smirked. "You find me irresistible."

She blinked a few times, then scoffed and gave his shoulder a shove. "Do not."

His smirk only widened as he watched her march toward the pasture where she'd already deposited their stallion. Her hips danced with each step she took, and he bit down on his fist as he allowed himself to enjoy the view.

One day she was going to look back on this moment and realize she'd been a fool to keep him at arm's length. They were made for each other. He just had to figure out a way to help her see that.

The rest of the day went as well as he'd hoped. Sophia didn't attempt to find excuses for leaving his side, and they joked about their matchmaking skills with the horses. When all the love birds were returned to their stalls, he found himself just hanging out with her on her front porch steps.

"Tell me something real," she said, not looking at him.

"Something real?" Cameron rubbed at the scruff along his jaw. "Like what?"

She peeked at him over her shoulder. "I dunno. Something you haven't told anyone else before."

He gave her a wry look. "You first."

She rolled her eyes and moved to get to her feet, but his hand grasped her wrist and he tugged her back to sit beside him.

"Fine, I'll tell you something."

Interest lit up her eyes, and he smirked.

"My favorite vegetable is broccoli."

She stared at him for a moment, then groaned as she rose to her feet again.

In no time at all, he snatched her wrist again. "Okay, okay. Something real."

Sophia didn't seem to believe that he was going to follow through this time around, and she didn't lower herself back to where she'd been sitting.

"My brother stole my first girlfriend from me."

Her eyes widened, and it was as if he'd doused her with a bucket of ice water at the shock on her face. "You're kidding."

Slowly, he shook his head. It had been years, and it was one of the main reasons he hated seeing the girl he liked in the arms of anyone else but him. He could admit that to himself, but he'd never admit that to anyone else. Telling Sophia this little tidbit felt like he was giving a piece of himself to her.

Cameron rubbed the back of his neck and fought the embarrassment. He wasn't angry with his brother over it anymore. And that girl was probably married with a bunch of kids by now. He simply had never gotten over the fact that he couldn't keep the attention of the first girl he'd tried to win over.

Sophia lowered herself to her seat at his side. "That really..." She shook her head. "I'm sorry, Cameron."

He shrugged and forced a smile that he didn't feel like giving her. "It was ages ago."

"Doesn't mean it doesn't matter," she said. Her eyes traced over him, scanning him from head to toe. "I bet that sort of thing doesn't happen anymore, huh?"

Cameron snorted. "No, I don't suppose it does." He didn't miss the desire that all but poured from her body. The way she leaned in. The way her tongue peeked out of her mouth to moisten her lips. Even the hitch in her breathing told him exactly what she thought about him. The chemistry he had with her was off the charts, and now that she knew he could be vulnerable with her, maybe they'd start making progress toward something again.

His fingertips traced lightly along her cheekbone as he brushed strands of hair behind her ear. "Your turn," he murmured beneath his breath. "Tell me something real."

She exhaled with a trembling breath. "I don't have anything to tell you."

He tsked. "Tit for tat, Red. Tell me something you haven't told anyone else."

Sophia closed her eyes and leaned into his touch.

"Why don't you date?" he whispered.

Her eyes flung wide, and she stiffened before jumping to her feet. "Pass."

Cameron watched her dart up to the front door and sighed. He should have asked her for something else.

WHY WAS it that he always ended up at this club on the weekends?

Because of *her*.

Sophia wasn't the type to sit still. She wasn't willing to commit to one person, and it showed in the way she flirted mercilessly with any guy who was halfway decent looking and gave her a smile.

Cameron had danced with her once tonight, but it was

difficult to keep her attention on him. He could feel the familiar tug of jealousy in his chest any time she let a guy pull her close. But the second the dance was over, she was on to another group of people. She didn't have any connections with any of them, and only one of them seemed interested in tugging her outside to see if he had a chance at something more.

Cameron had stopped that one real fast.

He arched a brow as that guy returned to Sophia's side and pulled her onto the dance floor. It was a slow song, and every few minutes, Sophia's eyes locked with Cameron. One side of his mouth quirked upward. She had the attention of more men than he had the attention of women, and yet he could see a familiar jealous streak in her own behavior when he danced with one of them.

The man she danced with attempted to take advantage of their proximity, his mouth dangerously close to the hollow of her neck. Cameron pushed off the wall and strode toward them. She hadn't kissed anyone since he'd arrived, and that was one thing he wasn't willing to let happen. He had no right, and yet he couldn't stop himself.

His hand landed on the guy's shoulder, and the man turned with recognition in his gaze. "Hey, man, we're busy—"

"I'm cutting in," Cameron interrupted, pushing the man to the side and scooping Sophia into his arms.

"Cam—" she started indignantly, but her words were cut off as he spun her away from her partner then back towards himself, so she collided with his chest. Her eyes were wide and bright with exhilaration. "What are you doing?" she breathed.

Cameron's mouth shifted to her ear. "Tell me something,

Sophia. How can you live with yourself?" His voice was teasing and light. He loved being with her this way.

She reared back. "What?"

"What makes you think that you can tempt me, tease me, then deny me?"

She made an attempt to pull away, but he held her tight, his voice growing huskier.

"You flirt mercilessly with any guy who looks your way, but then you stare daggers at any girl who attempts to flirt with me." He hit the nail on the head with that one. Her eyes widened further, and her cheeks flamed with color.

"I—you—that's not..."

He chuckled, not missing the way goosebumps rose on her arms. "Let me ask you something else. Why won't you let me get close to you... when you clearly don't want anyone else to get close to me?"

She worked her jaw, her eyes sharpening for a moment before she gave him a gentle shove. "You don't know what you're talking about," she said flippantly before making her escape.

13

———

Sophia

"I can't believe him!" Sophia groaned as she paced in front of her friend.

Emma laughed. "That's funny because I thought he made some good points."

Sophia whirled around and glowered at her friend. "What points? He hasn't made any points."

Her friend snickered again. "Think about it, Soph. He's cleared up the confusion with what happened in Texas, and he's still clearly interested. You can't tell me you don't like him back. Otherwise you wouldn't be acting this way."

"Acting what way?" Sophia muttered as she dropped into a chair on the porch. "I'm not doing anything I haven't been doing since you've met me." When Emma didn't respond right away, Sophia glanced at her once more. The pointed look she gave her was enough for Sophia to demand, "What?"

Emma shrugged. "You don't really believe that, do you?"

Sophia bit down on her lower lip before she frowned. Was she so easy to read?

"You like him."

Sophia scoffed.

"You really like him," Emma sang.

"What's not to like? He's charming, and he's attractive."

"*But...*" Emma drawled.

There were no "buts." Sophia and Emma both knew it. The problem wasn't with Cameron; it was with Sophia. She swallowed hard and peeked at her. "He's my friend."

Emma snorted, earning a sharp look from Sophia. "You keep telling yourself that. Seriously, Sophia. The guy is so your type. He's tall, built, and has just enough of an accent to make a girl's legs weak. I don't understand why you can't just give him a chance. And don't tell me that you're not interested in anything serious. No one wants to be alone forever. Not even you."

"I can't." The words slipped past Sophia's lips before she realized it.

"Why?" Emma pressed. "What aren't you telling me?"

Sophia had never said a word about her experiences to anyone. She hated the idea of pity more than anything else.

"Soph... if you don't want to tell me, it's okay... but maybe it would be nice to get it off your chest."

Emma made a good point. It would be nice to have someone in her corner.

She leaned over and rested her face in her hands. "It's not in the cards, Emma. Guys just don't stick around."

"Guys... or one guy specifically?"

Sophia grimaced. "Fine. One guy. He... apparently, I wasn't enough for him. He was my first really serious boyfriend, and instead of breaking up with me, he went behind my back and dated other girls." She could feel the pity coming from Emma, and she hated it. Her hands clenched as she lifted her gaze to her friend. "Don't feel bad for me."

Emma frowned. "I can feel bad for you because that's not something anyone should experience."

"Well, don't pity me."

"It's not pity, Soph. It's love."

Sophia shook her head and got to her feet. "He was always a big flirt. I think it was something that brought us together. The banter we had with each other was next level. I just never thought that he'd use his prowess to chase after someone else when we were still dating."

"I'm so sorry, Sophia."

"Yeah, well, that's life. And it happened long enough ago that it shouldn't matter."

Emma's hand reached out and took Sophia's hand in hers. "It will always matter. It just won't always hurt."

Sophia lifted her eyes toward her friend, fighting the tears that threatened to escape.

"But don't forget that Cameron isn't that guy."

"I know he isn't," Sophia muttered.

"Then don't treat him like he is. Cameron is trying to—"

"He's a lot like him, though. The way he flirts with me and pushes my buttons... sometimes it's all I can see."

Emma's frown deepened. "I'd be a hypocrite if I told you that you need to get over it. We all have our triggers."

"So, you're not going to tell me to just give in and open my heart to him?"

"As much as I want to? No. But I will ask you something. If

there is a chance for happiness with him, don't you think you owe it to yourself to try? Would the risk be worth the hurt? Cameron isn't the same guy as the one who betrayed you, and just because there are parts of him that remind you of that experience doesn't mean it will end the same. Maybe it will work. Maybe it won't. Either way, you won't know unless you try."

Sophia stared at where Emma's warm hand held her own. There was comfort in the way they were connected, and she couldn't deny that Emma had made a good point. As often as Sophia had told everyone and herself that she wasn't cut out for something serious, there was still a part of her that wanted it more than she would ever admit to anyone else. "Yeah, maybe."

"Maybe?" Emma grinned, releasing her.

"Yeah. Maybe." Sophia moved closer to her friend and pulled her in for a hug. They clung to each other for a few moments before Sophia pulled back. "Thanks."

"I didn't do anything." Emma laughed.

Sophia grinned. "You did more than you realize."

Sophia couldn't get Emma's advice out of her head as she went to work the following day. She was on edge for a completely different reason than before. The small part of her that still wanted to find love was growing.

She didn't want to end up alone.

And if Cameron was the guy who could make her happy? Then would it be so bad if she opened a door and gave him a chance? That thought was utterly terrifying if she were honest with herself. And yet, there was a small thrill that she'd only felt a handful of times since Brent had broken her heart.

It wasn't a surprise that Cameron was up and already at work. He was wandering down the barn aisle toward the mares he'd been observing. From where she stood in the doorway, she couldn't hear the things he was murmuring to them, but it still brought a smile to her face.

He was really good with the horses. She'd seen the way they took to him, trusting him easier than they'd trusted most newcomers. Mateo had done the right thing in hiring him, even if she'd been thrown for a loop by the revelation of it all.

Cameron paused before turning and facing her. The smile he gave her stirred the electricity that she'd grown to associate with being near him. If he had been upset with the way she'd bailed on him the last time they'd been together, he wasn't showing it.

Shoving her hands into her back pockets, she wandered toward him. "What's on the schedule today?"

He drew closer to her, meeting her partway. "Now that we know our stud and our mares get along, we have to wait for the girls to go into heat. For now, I'm monitoring their health—their exercise and eating habits."

She nodded. Ever since he'd shown up, he had taken hold of the reins and dictated what the horses needed, but he didn't get to decide all of it. "Tilly needs to go for a ride today. She's getting antsy," she said. "I'm guessing Birdie needs one, too." Sophia waited for him to argue with her. But he didn't. Instead, he glanced over his shoulder toward the horses briefly. "I think that's a good idea. Nothing too strenuous."

"Of course not," Sophia said. "I'll go easy on them." She

watched him for a moment. Most of what she knew about him was surface level—well, besides the story about his brother. She could tell he was passionate about his job, and people who could give that much of themselves to one thing had a tendency to spread that passion elsewhere.

The heat in her chest burned hotter and she moved closer to him. "Maybe you'd like to come along for a ride?"

He arched a brow. "Are you asking me on a date, Red?"

She rolled her eyes even as she bit back a smile. "In your dreams. Come if you want or don't."

The way he was watching her put her on edge in the most delicious way. She didn't want to admit that his decision mattered to her, but in all likelihood, he could already see that it did.

"Oh, I'm coming," Cameron purred. "And maybe you'll finally tell me something real."

Her heart stalled for a moment, then she flipped her hair as she brushed past him to head for the saddles. "Maybe."

The horses plodded along the trail, and Sophia could feel Cameron's stare each and every time he glanced in her direction. She bit down on her lower lip and looked at him. "You want something real?"

Cameron didn't say anything, but the look in his eye said he was on the edge of his seat.

"My hair used to be down to my waist. I grew it out as long as I could because I wanted to be a princess."

His brows lifted. She'd kept it short since she'd found out about Brent's treachery, so it wasn't a surprise that he couldn't envision it.

Sophia tilted her head forward so the short strands could hide some of her face. This was the first time she'd admitted this out loud. "After a particularly bad experience, I couldn't take it anymore. I didn't feel like a princess any longer, and I needed a change. So, I chopped it as short as I could and added some fire." She pinched some of the strands of red that she could see out of the corner of her eye. "My brothers freaked out." She let out a laugh. "I'd never done anything rebellious and then just walked in the door one day looking nothing like myself. I changed up my clothing style, too."

When she looked at him again, she found his mouth hanging open, but when he noticed her stare, he closed it.

"I know," she murmured. "It's silly, and I guess I shouldn't have—"

In a flash, he urged his horse into a trot that put him in her path, forcing her to pull up short. Her horse whinnied, and she frowned at him. "What's wrong?"

Cameron stared at her with nothing but understanding in his gaze. He shook his head. "It's not silly. Our experiences change us—usually on the inside. But sometimes that's not enough. Yours happened to transform you on the outside, too. Don't ever second guess the way your heart needed to cope."

It was almost like he knew exactly what she'd been through, and she wasn't sure she liked that feeling. But he couldn't—not unless he knew Brent personally. Her ex hadn't exactly kept his prowess a secret. Apparently, he'd shared his indiscretions with his friends as if being a cheater made him special.

"Sophia." Her name on his tongue sounded sweeter than it really should have, and she focused on him. She almost expected him to ask about her experience, but he didn't. "Whatever you're thinking, stop. Changing your hair isn't a sign of weakness. It's a sign of survival—of strength. You came out of whatever it was on top. Wear it like armor."

She stared at him with surprise. Now she really thought he might have an inkling of what she'd been through. Would he admit to it? Probably not. Then again, their conversation was so vague that she was likely overthinking all of this.

Sophia nodded her thanks, and Cameron moved out of the way so they could continue their ride.

14

———

Cameron

Cameron glanced at Sophia as he brushed down Tilly. Clearly, she didn't want him to know about her ex. If it hadn't been for her sister, he would never have guessed. He had started kicking himself the second she'd told him the story of why she'd chosen her particular hairstyle. Calling her Red might have dredged up memories she would rather not relive.

She glanced up at him, and in that moment, the world fell away. At least he hadn't put his foot in his mouth when she'd made her confession. She didn't seem upset about his reaction.

"Thanks," he said.

One side of her mouth lifted in a half-smile. "What for?"

"For telling me something real," he said simply.

Her smile widened. "Tit for tat, right?"

Cameron matched her smile with one of his own. He

moved toward her, boxing her into the corner of the stall. He pressed both of his palms against the wall over her shoulders and relished knowing how he was affecting her.

Sophia's chest rose and fell with more effort than before. She tilted her head up so her eyes found his and they practically sparkled as her cheeks filled with color. "Cameron," she whispered, her voice holding a note of warning.

"Hmm?" he murmured, leaning closer.

"Is there something you want?"

"There are a lot of things that I want, but I'd be ecstatic if you'd help me out with something."

"Oh? What is that?"

"How about a kiss?"

Her lips parted, and she blinked at him for a few moments before her eyes dipped to his mouth. She was going to do it. Sophia was finally going to give in and kiss him again. He shifted closer to her, and just before his lips were about to meet hers, she ducked out from beneath his arms and darted out of the stall.

By the time he turned around, she was halfway to the entrance of the barn. And when he stepped out into the aisle, she had disappeared out the door. He dragged a hand down his face. For someone who was so outgoing and flirtatious with the men who couldn't manage to stay away, this woman seemed to have the hardest time letting Cameron get close.

The sound that burst from his chest was a combination of a growl and a groan. He stalked back to the horses to finish up what he'd been doing. But before he lost himself completely in his work, his phone buzzed in his back pocket.

Cameron yanked it out and nearly dropped it into the straw at his feet when he saw the message. He'd gotten

Sophia's number when he'd started working at the ranch, but they'd only ever messaged one another for work.

This was definitely not work-related.

SOPHIA: *You might get your kiss if you take me on a date.*

THERE WASN'T an ounce of hesitation in Cameron's mind when he responded less than one minute later.

CAMERON: *Deal.*

HE GRINNED when she responded just as quickly.

SOPHIA: *Sal's. Tomorrow at seven.*

THE DINER WASN'T what he would have picked, especially since he'd never been able to take her on that second date he'd planned on five years ago.

CAMERON: *Nope. I'm planning this one. You owe me.*

SOPHIA: *Fine.*

.   .   .

CAMERON: *You just rolled your eyes, didn't you?*

SOPHIA: *Wouldn't you like to know?*

CAMERON: *I'll pick you up tomorrow at seven.*

SOPHIA: *Looking forward to it.*

NOTHING and no one would be able to wipe the smile from his lips.

~

"SO WHAT'S it gonna be? Dinner and a movie?"

Cameron gave Sophia a flat look. "With how hard it's been to get you to agree to this date, I wouldn't dream of it."

Sophia looped her arm into his. "Okay. Impress me."

It had taken him all day to decide where he was going to take Sophia so he'd make the best impression on her. As it stood, he wasn't sure if he'd made the right decision, but it was too late to go back now.

Copper Creek was an old town. There were historical buildings all over the place, and some had decent stories behind them. But there was one story that had caught his attention the second he'd heard it.

Cameron opened the door to his truck and motioned for Sophia to climb inside. She smirked at him. "Such a gentleman."

"Only the best for you."

Today was already a success just because of the way she smiled at him. He drove them to a less busy part of town. There was an older building that was surprisingly still standing after there had been a fire. A pottery studio still used the property, which was probably what made the place so special.

Sophia frowned when he pulled up to the front of the store. He might not be a local in the typical sense, but based on what he'd learned from Mateo, neither was his family. That fact gave him the confidence he needed to assume Sophia didn't know about what made this place special.

"A pottery studio? Are you a closet crafter, Cameron?"

He grinned at her. "Not hardly, though if you'd like to go inside and paint something, I won't complain."

She snorted. "I'm not exactly the pottery type, either." The curiosity burned in her eyes, but she didn't plead with him to tell her why they were there. He hurried around the front of the truck to help her out, but she was already halfway out by the time he got there.

Cameron frowned. "I was going to—"

"I'm not a princess, remember?" Sophia folded her arms. "I don't need you to open the door for me."

He wanted to argue but thought better of it. Instead of pointing out that a man should be able to treat a lady well, he slipped his hand into hers and led her to the sidewalk. She bumped into him as if she intended on going to the front door, but he took a beeline for the side of the building and guided her toward a less busy alleyway.

Before she could ask him what they were doing in the alley, she stopped short. Her eyes trailed over the backside of the building. The bricks still showed signs of being scorched, but as the original building was still standing, the owners had made the best of the situation. A bright, colorful mural covered the damage. Apparently, the owners of the place didn't want to pay to paint over the damage. The community had come together to create something new.

"What happened here?" she said.

"A fire."

"I can see that," she said with a laugh. "But what's all this?" She gestured to the images painted on the building. Nothing about the mural was cohesive except for the fact that the people of this town had chosen to represent themselves. Horses, nature, other animals, and a beautiful sunset made this wall a work of art.

Cameron turned his attention to Sophia while she drank it in. "The owners of this pottery studio went through something horrific. They lost so much, but miraculously, most of the building survived." He continued to watch her, waiting for her to realize the significance of why he'd brought her here. "Instead of spending their money to replace the exterior with new bricks or painting over it with the typical brick color, they brought the community together. The scars are still present, but so is the evidence of their strength."

Sophia frowned as her focus darted to him, still not understanding what he was getting at.

"Do you think that painting over those scorch marks shows weakness?"

"Of course not..." she hedged.

He reached out and touched the red strands of her hair. Understanding dawned on her face and she blinked several times as emotion showed in her eyes. Cameron didn't have to say anything more, but he did. "And neither does this." He tucked her hair behind her ear.

For a moment he considered kissing her. But the moment didn't feel quite right. Sophia broke their eye contact first when she grabbed his hand and tugged him toward the entrance of the alley.

"Come on. I want to take you somewhere."

Cameron grinned as she pulled him along. He'd had more plans for them, but he got the distinct feeling that this would be better.

"Turn here."

Cameron gave Sophia a side-eyed stare, then he smirked. Signs for the fair had been plastered all along this highway. He'd been aware that there was a fair in town, and he'd seriously considered recreating their first date. But after she'd shared the story about her choice in hairstyle, he'd known he needed something better.

He didn't dare hope that she had a similar idea—nor that they could be even more perfectly matched. But if she did, then that would solidify everything he knew to be true.

The smile on her face was so like the smiles she'd given him back in Texas when they'd first met. She seemed freer with this one. It wasn't a mask of who she thought everyone wanted her to be. With him, she was real.

When she directed them into the overfilled parking lot, he just knew it. She was going to take him up to the Ferris wheel, and they were going to look at the stars.

"What?" she demanded, and he blinked. Shoot, how long had he been staring? He shook his head, and she rolled her eyes. "Come on, let's go." True to Sophia fashion, she didn't allow him to open the door for her. By the time he got out of the truck and to her side, she was already striding toward the entrance to the fairgrounds.

Cameron slipped his hand into hers, and she didn't pull away. His heart hammered in his chest when she gave his hand a little squeeze. He must be a complete sap. Already he could see a future with this woman. She had enchanted him from the moment he met her, and she still made him want to learn all he could about her.

His desire for her only increased when they got in line for the Ferris wheel. The smile on his face must have been all sorts of ridiculous because Sophia squeezed his hand again as she looked up at him. "What are you thinking?"

He shook his head and brought her hand to his lips. "If you knew what was going on in my head," he murmured against her skin, "it would scare you off." Cameron almost expected her to pull away at his confession. Heck, he had anticipated that she'd look nervous or demand that he expound on what he'd said.

But she didn't.

Her expression was thoughtful, and if he wasn't mistaken, there was a hint of amusement toying at her lips. It almost disappointed him that she didn't demand that he explain himself. There would be plenty of time for that later.

At the top of the Ferris wheel, she looked at the stars while he was happy to look at her.

"You know something?" she said as the Ferris wheel came to a halt to allow people to get on and off. "I'd never ridden a Ferris wheel before that day you took me on one."

He scoffed. "I don't believe that for a second."

She turned to him with a laugh. "It's true. That was the first time."

He studied her, not seeing any lie in her eyes. "Why? Didn't you do that sort of thing as a kid?"

Sophia shrugged. "Never thought that the Ferris wheel would be fun. I thought it looked... boring."

Cameron couldn't help it. He tossed his head back with a laugh. "Of course you did. You don't strike me as the sort of person who does anything by halves. Let me guess. You preferred the rides that set your heart racing."

"Exactly," she said with a smile, but then it fell away and her gaze turned serious. "You ruined me, you know."

"What?"

"You ruined me for other guys. Every date I went on, I compared it to that one."

He didn't know whether to be heartbroken for her or intrigued by where she was going with this conversation. He could sense she was nervous, and the best thing would be to lighten the mood. Leaning close, he murmured, "I thought you didn't date."

Sophia snickered and pushed at his chest. "No second dates."

"Except with me."

Her eyes flicked up to meet his for a long moment. "Except with you," she agreed.

Man, how his heart soared at that comment. "Does that mean you'll agree to go out with me again?"

The Ferris wheel lurched forward, and she clutched his hand a little harder. Sophia chewed on her lower lip, tilting her head to the side for a moment before nodding. "I don't know. It's gonna be hard to top this one."

He groaned with exaggeration. "Don't break my heart, Red—" Cameron cleared his throat and rubbed the back of his neck. "Sorry, I guess I shouldn't call you that..."

She leaned forward so her lips nearly grazed his ear. "I like it." Then she moved to his cheek and brushed a whisper of a kiss to its surface. "And I'd love to go out with you again."

Pulling back to make sure he heard her right, he searched her eyes for any indication she was pulling his leg but saw none. A smile tugged at his lips, but the fear was still rooted deep in his gut. "Do I need to be worried that you're going to disappear for five years?"

Sophia released a laugh and swatted at him, but he caught her wrist before she could make contact. Her eyes locked with his as he tugged her closer.

"Because this time, I know where you live," he whispered huskily, "and it's gonna be harder to escape me now that I have you in my sights." His eyes dipped to her mouth before lifting to her eyes. She nodded. Then he closed the distance between them as he brushed a kiss to her lips.

The tease of his skin against hers was excruciatingly delicious and he wanted more, but he forced himself to hold back.

Sophia stared up at him with surprise, and he gave her his most charming grin. "Just in case we don't get that date you promised me."

15

———

Sophia

That kiss.

Goodness gracious, that kiss had been something she'd never experienced before. It had been sweet and hot all at once, and he'd barely even touched her.

Sophia's skin practically buzzed as she grabbed the coffee mug that she'd just filled with her favorite brew. The rest of their date the night before had been perfect. They'd played a few games, and Cameron had won her a stuffed horse. He got her a deep-fried Twinkie, and it almost felt like they had been together for years instead of... well, instead of the two dates they'd been on.

Mateo entered the kitchen and yawned. It was early yet, but Sophia figured Cameron would already be out in the barn making the rounds. She smiled at the thought of seeing him and couldn't help but wonder what he would plan for their next date.

Maybe she should be the one to pick their outing. Then again, she had a tendency to pick the same old things. She couldn't help it if she enjoyed dancing and eating junk food. Those were her comforts.

And yet, she had absolutely felt seen when he'd taken her to that pottery studio.

"What's that grin about?" Mateo asked, his brow arching.

Her eyes widened slightly, and she peered at her brother over the edge of her mug. "What? Nothing."

"Right," he drawled. "Please tell me that you're not messing with Cameron. I know he has a contract and all, but I'd really rather he didn't get his heart broken."

She nearly coughed on the inhale of coffee she'd been intent on drinking. "What? Why would you say that?"

Her brother's pointed look said it all. He knew that she didn't have any intention of settling down. She didn't do second dates, even though he had mentioned that she ought to give a couple of the guys she'd been out with more of a chance. What would he say if he knew that she was finally open to something more—and with none other than the guy he'd just hired?

Mateo frowned. "Sophia," he warned.

Giving him her most innocent smile, she batted her lashes. "What?"

"You need to steer clear of the guys who work for me. I don't want it to get messy."

She huffed a laugh. "You're not the boss of me."

"Technically, I am. And I'm his boss, too. Just do me a favor and keep it clean, okay?"

The temptation to roll her eyes and fight back was a strong one. Mateo had a good point. Cameron hadn't been working for them long. And it would be complicated if he was forced to stick around if things didn't work out between the two of them.

"Is that a yes?"

She glanced at her brother briefly. "You know me. I'm not interested in anything serious." It wasn't the answer he was asking for. And he knew she could flirt up a storm if she wanted to. Hopefully, he wouldn't notice that something had changed between herself and their most recent hire. Sophia placed her nearly empty mug into the sink. "I'm going to get to work."

Thankfully, Mateo didn't question her further. He could read her better than most, and she wasn't ready to admit that Cameron had been the first guy to get past her defenses since Brent had broken her heart.

The second she saw Cameron, her heart did that fluttering thing she hadn't experienced in five years. He flashed her a smile, and for the first time in a long time, her returning smile was automatic.

"Hey," she murmured.

"Hey." He moved past her to get something off a shelf, and his hand brushed against hers. Sparks flickered up her arm from the contact, and she shivered.

"I've got some training exercises I want to do with some of the horses. Will that be a problem?" she asked.

Cameron glanced at her and shook his head. "Nope. As long as it's not too strenuous."

"Nothing they can't handle." She set to work gathering the lead ropes she'd need for the horses she planned on taking out to the corral. It was impossible to keep track of how many times she felt Cameron's eyes on her. Each time she did, she'd glance at him and catch him staring.

More than once, she caught herself smiling at the attention, and she shook her head. They were grown adults, and yet it felt like she'd gone back in time to when she'd been a hormonal teenager. She found she wanted any excuse to get close to him, to smell his cologne and to hold his hand.

But they had work to do. Both of them.

The beautiful golden-brown horse trotted around the perimeter of the corral, tossing her head as she let out a happy whinny. Her muscles bunched and flexed perfectly. If she wasn't a working horse, she would have been perfect for dressage.

Sophia clicked her tongue and flicked her whip to the ground with a crack to get the horse moving a little faster. This creature was the perfect specimen for breeding, and they were going to get beautiful offspring if all went well.

Her eyes lifted at the sound of boots crushing against the gravel. One of the wranglers that Mateo had hired darted up to the corral, colliding with it. He was out of breath and his eyes were wide with concern. "Where's Mateo?"

Sophia frowned. The last she'd seen him, he'd left in his truck to run a few errands. "I don't know, but I can call him for you."

He nodded. "It's urgent."

Sophia moved to unlatch the lead rope from the horse she was working with and pulled out her phone. "What's going on? Is someone hurt?" Her brothers had been out working on bringing the cattle back from the farthest pasture they owned. "Are Roman and Marcus—"

"They're fine," he barked. "But you need to call Mateo so he can come out to the northern pasture."

She nodded, her hands shaking slightly as she dialed her brother's number.

"Yeah," he muttered the second he answered.

Sophia's eyes shifted to the cowboy, and she sucked in a deep breath before exhaling. "Something's wrong in the northern pasture."

"What's the matter?" The alarm in his voice carried through the speaker loud enough to prompt the cowboy in front of her to offer more of an explanation. "Wolf attack."

She exhaled sharply. "Wolf attack," she repeated.

Her brother swore under his breath. "I'll be there as soon as I can."

Sophia nodded, her eyes darting to the cowboy. "He'll be here as soon as he can." The cowboy spun around and headed back the way he'd come. Mateo's voice drew her back.

"They're getting closer."

"The wolves?" she asked.

"Yeah." He sighed. "The sheriff said that they've been attacking the livestock on the outskirts of town. I thought we were close enough that they wouldn't come to our property, but I guess—"

"This wasn't the first one, though."

"Yeah," Mateo said, "I know. We might have to send out patrols at night." He sighed again. "Look, we're not going to panic until there is an official sighting. They might still stay on the outskirts of the property. We're just going to have to keep an eye on it—keep our herds safe."

"So, you don't want me to tell anyone else? I'm sure the guys—"

"I'll talk to them myself when I get there. What pasture were they at?"

Sophia glanced at the cowboy's retreating form again. "They said the northern pasture."

Mateo grunted. There were other voices in the background, and it sounded like he might be at a coffee shop or some other small business. "I'll see you when I get back. We'll have a family meeting about this and decide what's going to be best."

"I'll make sure Daniel knows he's included, then."

"Thanks, Sophia."

She hung up the phone with a distinct level of trepidation. The wolves had been a nuisance over the last couple of years, but they had been easy to scare off according to some of the other ranchers. But the pack was getting braver. Not only had a neighboring pasture had an attack, now one of Mateo's animals had been attacked. If something wasn't done, this would only get worse.

Her phone rang and she paused, seeing Mateo's number on the screen.

"Yes?" she asked, placing the phone to her ear.

"I hate to ask this of you on short notice, but with the wolf issue and some other things I have to take care of, I can't watch Paxton while Nikki is out tonight."

Sophia frowned. She'd planned on spending time with Cameron. They didn't have an *official* plan in mind besides that, but she'd been excited to make up for lost time. She could almost guarantee that he had something fun up his sleeve because that was just who he was.

"Sophia?"

"Yeah, okay. I can do it."

"Thanks." His breath of relief did nothing to ease the disappointment she felt in having to tell Cameron they'd be postponing any shenanigans. He'd understand. That was the kind of guy Cameron was.

"You owe me, though," Sophia said just as the phone disconnected.

Arms came around her and she gasped as she spun to face the intrusion. Cameron's eyes clashed with hers, desire laced within them. "I was thinking. We should go dancing tonight."

She opened her mouth to explain why that wasn't going to happen when he cut her off with a finger to her lips.

"I know I haven't had the best track record at that club you like going to so much, but I thought that seeing as I will be the one to escort you there, we won't have any trouble with strangers pulling you close in order to steal your attention from me and vice versa."

His proposition sounded so nice. She loved going dancing, and knowing that Cameron would be there as her date sent her heart into all sorts of acrobatics. Her eyes must have given her away, and he released her as he stepped back. "What's wrong."

The lack of his touch practically burned her. "I can't."

Her disappointment was mirrored in his gaze, but there was something else hovering just beneath the surface. He was upset with her—no, not just upset. Was he actually angry? "Don't tell me that you're running from me, Red. Not again."

"What?" she demanded. "I'm *not* running."

"What do you expect me to believe? We kiss and suddenly—"

Understanding flooded her being. "I didn't say I didn't *want* to."

His mouth snapped shut, and the look of confusion was enough to make her laugh.

"Wow, I must have done a number on you." She moved toward him, and to her relief he didn't back away. She draped her arms around his neck. "I would love nothing more than to go dancing with you. My favorite place to be is in your arms, Cameron. Don't ever forget that."

His hands found her waist, and he pulled her closer. A deep red color crawled up his neck and settled in his ears as he gave her a sheepish smile. "I'm sorry," he said with a grimace. "I don't know what got into me."

She placed a hand to his cheek. "It's fine. I'd practically agreed to do something with you this morning and I was just about to come find you to tell you I'm needed here."

His brows pulled together. "Here?"

Sophia nodded. "There's been a wolf attack in our herd. Mateo has to deal with that and do some other stuff, so he can't watch his son while his wife is out. He wanted me to keep an eye on my nephew."

She didn't think it was possible, but Cameron's face turned a deeper shade of red. He dragged a hand down his face. "I'm such a jerk."

Laughter spilled from her lips. "You just overreacted a little. It's okay. Rain check?"

He nodded. "Rain check."

16

Cameron

Cameron stood outside Sophia's house later that night with a grocery bag full of everything he could think of to make tonight special. He wanted to make things right between them. His blunder still hung in the air, and he didn't want Sophia to think that this was who he was. He could be jealous, sure. And sometimes he jumped the gun. But he refused to lose her because of his flaws. There were good sides to him, too.

He knocked, and when the door opened, he was surprised to see Roman behind it. Roman frowned, his eyes taking Cameron in from head to toe. "You probably shouldn't be here."

Cameron rolled his eyes. "Just let me in. I know Mateo isn't here. Sophia is babysitting, and I want to help."

Roman arched a single brow and folded his arms. "You want to babysit?"

"Just let him in," Sophia's voice called, and Cameron grinned.

Roman sighed. "All right. Fine. But if you hurt—"

Cameron brushed past him. "If I hurt her, then I'm dead meat. I get it."

The door shut behind Cameron. He found Sophia seated on the floor with a small boy in the front room. They were playing with some toy horses, and the television was on in the background.

Sophia cocked her head to the side, with that knowing smile gracing her lips and making him feel invincible while at the same time completely disarmed.

The bag in his hands suddenly felt like it weighed a ton, and he offered her a sheepish grin. "I thought you could use some backup."

She snickered. "Paxton is an angel. No backup needed."

He lifted the bag with a shrug. "I don't suppose the angel would be interested in a movie and some junk food?"

Paxton's eyes lit up like a Christmas tree. He glanced from Sophia back to Cameron before launching himself from the floor and rushing toward the bag of goodies. "What did you bring? Is there popcorn?"

"I wouldn't be very cool if I didn't have popcorn, would I?" Cameron smirked. His eyes shifted toward Sophia, and he found her watching him intently. Her eyes were guarded, so there wasn't much he could do to discern how she felt about him crashing her babysitting gig.

Then she smiled, and the world turned right-side-up.

He grinned back and moved farther into the room where he could put the bag down.

They pulled out six varieties of candy, popcorn, jerky, and a recent release of an animated film. Paxton insisted they needed to build a fort to watch the movie from and darted off to gather blankets while calling out to Cameron and Sophia to pull the cushions from the couch.

Sophia chuckled as she pulled the first one free and placed it on the floor. She cut him a glance out of the corner of her eye. "You're pretty good with kids."

"Thanks," he said.

"Do you have nieces and nephews?"

He shook his head. "Not yet. My brother doesn't seem inclined to settle down, so who knows if I ever will." He didn't bother mentioning that he wouldn't mind Paxton becoming his nephew if everything went the way he wanted it to with Sophia. The last thing he needed was to scare Sophia off.

There was a brief frown that marred her pretty face, and it had him wondering if she was recalling what he'd said of his brother and the history he had with him. But just as quickly as it had arrived, it disappeared.

Paxton returned before he could ask her about it.

In no time, they were all scrunched in beneath a fort constructed of chairs, cushions, and blankets. Paxton had picked the space between the two of them, and he was seated, hunched forward with his eyes glued to the television, which offered Cameron an unobstructed view of Sophia.

Every so often she'd glance in his direction, and he'd smile right back. Life couldn't get any better than it was at this moment. He could see a future with Sophia doing this exact activity with their own children.

Goodness. What was happening here? These were thoughts he'd never had with anyone else. But he knew in his heart, it was exactly what he wanted.

He reached for her hand and laced his fingers between hers behind Paxton's back. They had an undeniable connection, and there was nothing he wouldn't do to protect it. If he had to go to war for her, he would.

Soon enough, the movie ended, which meant bedtime for Paxton. Sophia excused herself to take care of the bedtime routine while Cameron put everything right again in the front room. Cushions were replaced, blankets were folded, and chairs returned to the kitchen. By the time Sophia had returned to him, the room looked good as new.

Cameron patted the seat beside him on the couch, and she settled against him. They were quiet for a long moment, just letting the silence of the evening wrap around them like a warm blanket. Nothing else was going on in the house. Her family were either still out or had turned in early.

Her head rested against his chest, and he brought his arm around her. Letting his fingers thread through her hair, he reveled in its soft texture. She'd changed her hair because of a bad experience, as a way to reinvent herself, and yet he couldn't imagine her any other way.

Sophia's thoughts must have taken a similar turn because she sighed. "My ex... his name was Brent." She sighed again. "He loved my long hair. He always said that it made me look like a princess in all those storybooks, and he wanted me to keep growing it out just to see how long I could get it."

Cameron tensed. Was this the boyfriend who had hurt her?

Thankfully, Sophia didn't seem to notice his reaction to her statement, and she continued. "His nickname for me was Princess, and every gift he gave, every card, anything revolving around us and our relationship was royalty themed. I loved it. He made me feel so special—like he saw me better than anyone else." She sucked in a deep breath and blew it out harshly. "Then I found out he was cheating on me with a couple different girls from other schools in nearby cities."

He couldn't help it. Despite knowing this confession was coming, Cameron couldn't contain the rage he felt on her behalf. One hand clenched tightly at his side, and he prayed she didn't notice the way he was reacting. She didn't like it when he got angry. But this was a serious issue. It didn't matter that it took place years ago. Someone had hurt her and made her feel like she was worthless.

"Anyway, that's why I cut it." She lifted her own hand to the strands surrounding her face. "That's why I needed the change. I didn't want to look anything like a princess. It made me sick to make that association." There was an edge to her voice he had only heard a handful of times since he'd met her. "I'm not some damsel in distress or some girl who needs saving. I'm not a princess."

Cameron shifted so he could see her face. "I've never thought you were some damsel who needed to be saved." He chuckled, his hand cupping her chin. "I doubt anyone would look at you and see that. You're strong, capable, and a spitfire to boot."

A smile tugged at her lips and her eyes dipped to his mouth like she wanted to kiss him for the compliment.

He moved closer if only to indicate that his thoughts were in a similar place. His voice grew husky, and his breath fanned her face as he murmured, "I would never hurt you like that, Red. You are everything to me." With that confession on his lips, he brushed a kiss on hers that was both scintillating and filled with all the promises he had yet to make.

She pushed her hands around his neck and into his hair as she clung to him. No words needed to be said after that. They had each other, and they both knew it. With how good it was to be in her arms, he couldn't think of anything more he could ever want.

A FEW MORE WEEKS PASSED, and they only got closer. Sophia shared parts of herself that she hadn't shared with anyone else. Cameron felt he knew her inside and out.

The way they had behaved toward one another in the beginning was ancient history. Together, they made a good team. Cameron could see himself settling down in a place like Copper Creek.

"You know, I've been wondering. What's going to happen when the contract with my brother is up?" Sophia hovered in the doorway of the stall where Cameron was doing a few tests to discern whether or not they'd successfully bred the mare in question.

He glanced over his shoulder at her, a smile tugging at his mouth. "Do my ears deceive me? Are you worried about my leaving?"

She scoffed, humor in her eyes, but at the same time he could see a marginal amount of trepidation. It had already been a few months and time was ticking. There had been some inquiries by other ranches for him to set up another contract, and he'd been putting them off. Normally, he would have the next one lined up, and yet he couldn't pull the trigger to do so.

He heaved a groan as he straightened to his full height and moved toward her. His fingers brushed the hair at her brow and slid until he tucked strands behind her ear. With his other hand, he pulled her close. "All you have to do is ask me to stay, Sophia. I won't go anywhere unless you want me to."

Her breaths were shallower now. His proximity had a tendency to do that to her. She stared at him for a few heart-wrenching moments, and he started to second-guess whether they had a relationship that was strong enough to withstand the storms most took on in a lifetime.

Then she put him out of his misery as she framed his face with both of her palms. "Stay."

His heart pounded. His stomach flipped. He hadn't called a single place home in over five years. "Really?" he whispered.

"Really," she murmured back. "Put down roots. Move to Colorado. I'm sure there's plenty of work for you to do within driving distance." Then she shrugged. "And maybe Mateo might consider hiring you on full-time." She blushed and nodded again. "I really want you to stay."

"Okay," he whispered, "but only because you're obsessed with me."

Sophia laughed and pushed him away before he had a chance to kiss her. "More like you're obsessed with me."

She wasn't wrong. He hadn't felt this way about anyone… ever. Sophia was the woman of his dreams. She had been since he'd seen her at that conference. He chuckled and got back to his work. He finished collecting the blood samples he'd be sending to the lab. Holding them up, he grinned. "In a few days we'll know if we have reason to celebrate."

17

Sophia

Sophia charged toward the wranglers' cabin with an envelope in her hand and a smile on her face. She hadn't opened the lab results yet because she wanted to share in the excitement with Cameron.

Being with him was so different than any other relationship she'd had. He was thoughtful and spontaneous. And part of her even liked that jealous streak he'd shown when they were in the beginning of their relationship.

He had been amazing with Paxton, and she could see a possible scenario where Cameron became the person she married.

But she was getting ahead of herself. Right now, they were enjoying themselves. They went out every weekend and spent time together, even if it was brief, in the evenings. He was the first smile she sought out every morning and the last one she wanted to see before bed.

Part of her wondered how things might have been different if she hadn't run from the heartache she'd had five years ago. Where would she and Cameron be if they had a chance from that first night?

Sophia had to shove that thought down deep. She was the one responsible for pushing him away when he'd had a reasonable explanation. Lessons had been learned, and she wasn't about to overreact again. Cameron hadn't deserved her overreaction. Now, she was going to take full advantage of what they had together.

She entered the wranglers' cabin and stopped in the common area. It was decorated tastefully with pictures of cowboys or cattle on every wall. The furniture was rustic, made of wood or leather. It was an open floor plan concept with a kitchen and sitting area off the entrance and a hallway leading to the bedrooms. There were a few men lounging in the area, eating food they'd brought back from the cafeteria, but no Cameron. She hadn't learned most of their names yet since she'd been spending most of her time with Cameron, but Jason was among them, and they'd gotten friendly enough whenever she visited Nikki in the kitchens.

Sophia nearly asked one of the men to check the back for Cameron, but Jason approached and spoke first. "Hey, Sophia. How's it going?"

She offered the cowboy a genuine smile. He helped Nikki in the kitchen most days, but lately he'd been taking on more responsibilities with the horses. "It's going well." She held up the letter. "We might have some good news today."

"Yeah?" Jason moved even closer, and she backed into the doorway. He lifted his arm and rested it above her head against the doorjamb, looking down at her with a grin. "What kind of news?"

She smirked if only to cover for the fact that his proximity didn't feel quite right. He was a naturally flirtatious guy, and up until this point, she hadn't thought anything of it. But now? She couldn't help but feel like it was a bit much. "Just waiting to see if Cameron's been successful with the breeding process. I don't know about you, but I wouldn't mind an excuse to go out tonight."

In a flash of movement, Jason was yanked away from her. Sophia gasped, and her eyes fell on an angry-looking Cameron. He was breathing heavier than he should have been and his hands were flexing and clenching at his sides. "Stay away from her," he growled.

"Cameron!" she admonished. "What are you doing?"

Jason looked more surprised than anything else. His eyes darted past Cameron to Sophia before landing back on Cameron. He raised his hands in a placating gesture. "Easy, man. I was just talking to her."

Before Cameron could say something he would likely regret, Sophia grabbed at his arm. "Hey. I was looking for you. We have a letter to open."

At that, Cameron turned to face her, and his hard eyes softened as they landed on her face. He glanced at the letter in her hand as a hint of a smile clawed at his lips. "Is that what I think it is?" he said.

She waved it at him, the tussle he'd nearly gotten himself into completely forgotten. "What do you think it is?" she cooed.

He pulled her close, their chests bumping. "I think it might be the reason I get to take you to dinner tonight."

Sophia shrugged. "Maybe." She pulled him back to the door, refusing to make eye contact with any of the guys who had witnessed his outburst. To be fair, the position she'd been in had likely looked scandalous. That was just how Jason was. She was sure he got himself into trouble with that behavior more often than not.

They exited the cabin and made their way into the cool evening air. When they got far enough from the building for Sophia to feel comfortable again, she pressed the envelope to Cameron's chest with a grin. "How about you do the honors?"

He took it. "It'll be my pleasure."

She watched as he painstakingly slipped his fingers into the paper and tore a line through the top of the envelope. Sophia groaned exaggeratedly. "If you don't get on with it, I'll steal your thunder and open it myself."

Cameron chuckled and pulled out the document. "Of the five specimens received, we can confirm that four of the results are positive." His boyish grin sent her heart into overdrive. "You hear that? Four out of five!" He pulled her into a hug and spun her around. "This definitely means we need to celebrate. Dinner?"

"I already ate." Sophia poked him in the chest. "And I'd wager you did too."

"Dancing?"

She frowned. "We went dancing last night."

He put her on her feet. "What should we do, then?

Sophia tapped her lips for a moment, and he gave her a wicked grin. "No, I'm not saying you kiss me," she said with an eye roll, though that wasn't a bad idea. "Let's go to town and play it by ear. There's a new bakery open that sells chocolates and ice cream. I wouldn't say no to a triple chocolate bit of goodness."

"Ice cream it is," Cameron whispered so close to her ear that it set off waves of goosebumps.

THE BAKERY WAS ADORABLE. It reminded Sophia of a place she used to go to where she grew up. Most tables were only big enough to hold two to four people. There was a display filled with different kinds of chocolates, truffles, or chocolate-covered goodies. There was another display across from the chocolates showcasing the ice cream options available, along with the toppings to go with them.

There were a good number of people in the shop already. Cameron released her hand and nodded to the only open table. "You get us a seat, and I'll get our treats. You still want triple chocolate?"

Her stomach growled in answer, and he chuckled.

Sophia settled into her seat to wait, and not even a few minutes passed before a guy approached. He rested his hands on the table and grinned. "Hey, Sophia. How are you doing?"

She couldn't place him, but that wasn't saying much. With how many guys she'd gone on dates with over the last couple of years, they had started to blur together. Sophia bit down on her lower lip and tilted her head. "I'm sorry. Do we know each other?"

He placed a hand to his chest with an exaggerated groan. "You wound me."

Sophia rolled her eyes with a laugh.

"It's Tanner. We went out about a year ago. Then I had to move to the city for a while." He ran a hand through his blond hair. "I'm back in town. What do you say we go out?"

She shook her head, but before she could say anything, he cut her off.

"Oh, yeah. You don't do second dates." He leaned even

closer, and his voice lowered. "But since it's been a year, maybe we could count this as a first date."

Sophia couldn't help the laugh that spilled from her lips. "Nice try, but I'm not interested. I'm sorta dating someone."

Tanner's brows lifted and he let out a whistle. "Must be some guy if he could convince you to change your mind."

She fidgeted, fighting the urge to look in Cameron's direction. "Yeah, he is."

The guy in front of her bounced back quick, thank goodness. He straightened, then winked. "Right, well, if you find you need a change, I'm working over on the Callahans' property."

"Thanks," Sophia said. "But I'm good." She watched him leave, then pulled out her phone when it vibrated. It was a message from Mateo. There hadn't been any more wolves on their property, but there was another attack on the ranch backed up to the east of theirs. He wanted to tighten the security at their ranch, which meant he'd be assigning the men to make rounds more frequently.

Ice cream landed before her, and she jumped, her head whipping up to find Cameron yanking out a chair and taking a seat. He looked decidedly less happy than he'd been when they entered the bakery.

Frowning, Sophia pulled her ice cream closer. "What's wrong? Did they not have what you wanted?"

He glanced away briefly, his jaw tightening. But then his irritated expression shifted to something softer when he turned his focus on her. "It's fine. I found something I wanted."

"Well, it's not much of a celebration if you don't get to enjoy it. Do you want to go somewhere else?"

Once again, he looked elsewhere, but she didn't catch

onto what he was staring at. She made up his mind for him as she got to her feet. "Tell you what. I'm going to use the restroom, and then we can take this stuff to go. You pick our next stop, and we can both have fun. Movies. Dancing. Whatever you want."

He smiled tightly at her and nodded.

Sophia squeezed his shoulder, then headed off for the bathroom. It was clean and the smell of the bakery permeated the space.

Two girls entered the bathroom just as Sophia was leaving and one of them said, "Can you believe that guy? Geez. I feel bad for whoever..."

Her voice faded as the door closed behind Sophia. When she entered the main part of the shop, Cameron wasn't seated at the table where she'd left him. Instead, he was talking to a couple of guys. The three of them looked to be in a tense conversation. What stood out to Sophia was the fact that not only was Cameron in the group, but Tanner was as well.

Cameron poked him in the chest. Tanner smirked, but the guy beside him gave Cameron a little shove. By the time she moved closer, the conversation was over and Cameron was stalking toward her.

"Everything okay?" she asked, her eyes finding Tanner. The cowboy winked at her but did nothing else.

"Yeah, peachy," Cameron said. "Get your ice cream. Let's go."

She hurried after him, falling into step at his side. "Are you sure? What did those guys do?"

"It doesn't matter," Cameron bit out. "Don't worry about it."

Sophia frowned but didn't press the issue. Maybe Tanner

had come up to him and said something about her after she'd gone. Cameron was protective. If he thought that Tanner was being inappropriate, she wouldn't put it past him to say something.

Cameron took her hand in his, pulling her to a stop. He studied her for a moment before he leaned in close and kissed her forehead. "I've got two options for us. Star gazing or bookstore."

Her brows lifted, and her smile returned. "Ooh. How could I possibly choose?"

"Both it is." He chuckled. And just like that, the tension was cleared away.

18

Cameron

Cameron had his reasons for confronting the cowboy at the chocolate shop. The guy was clearly coming onto her. Cameron had clocked the guy and his friend the second he'd entered the shop. He'd seen Sophia walk in with Cameron. He'd noticed that they were holding hands. He'd blatantly disregarded everything and hit on Sophia like he could steal her away.

If Sophia hadn't returned so quickly, Cameron wasn't sure that things wouldn't have escalated. What was it with people like his brother who thought they had the right to encroach on another's relationship? He would have never dreamed of coming between a girl and the guy she went out with.

Unless it was Sophia.

He shook that truth from his mind. Sophia was different. They were made for each other. He could see that plain as day, and if someone wanted to claim he was crazy or obsessed, he couldn't care less. Sophia's heart belonged to him, and his heart was irrevocably hers.

They'd spent plenty of time perusing the shelves in the local bookstore and then they headed out to the hills away from the lights of town so they could get a good look at the stars.

When it was just the two of them here like this, he was at peace. No one could make him feel so at ease. Sophia had a way about her that made him feel seen and cherished. Her attention remained on him, and it didn't matter if he stumbled over his words or made a fool of himself in other ways; she still looked at him like he was everything.

Currently, they were sprawled out on a blanket he'd pulled from the back of his truck and were staring up at the sky. Sophia rolled over and propped herself up on one elbow. "Tell me about your brother."

He frowned, which spurred her laughter.

"I know you two didn't have the best relationship in your later teenage years, but it couldn't have been *all* bad, could it?"

Cameron worked his jaw and shifted his focus to the darkened sky. He laced his fingers behind his head and heaved a sigh. "No, it wasn't all bad."

"So, tell me about him. The good parts."

He took in a deep breath before cutting a glance at Sophia out of the corner of his eye. "He's my older brother— just over a year older. We were friends with all the same people which was both good and bad." He let out a mirthless chuckle. "As you can imagine, there were moments when we were very competitive with one another. Sports. Grades. That sort of stuff. Up until he'd... intervened... in my relationship with my first girlfriend, he'd been there for me. He was a protective older brother in every sense of the word." A smile fell to his lips unbidden. "We were actually very close."

"But not anymore?"

He blew out a heavy breath. "No, not anymore. I hear from him on occasion, but we don't really see each other except at big family events. I don't even know if he realizes I'm so close."

She shot up. "Close?"

He chuckled ruefully. "Yeah. He relocated to Colorado Springs about the time you and I met."

Sophia was quiet for a long moment. She chewed on her lower lip. "I can't imagine my siblings doing anything to betray me so thoroughly. I don't blame you for your feelings toward him. But at the same time, he's your only brother. And what happened... it's been years."

Cameron shrugged. "He's got his life, and I've got mine. We're cordial. That's good enough."

She scrunched up her face in the most adorable expression that he'd seen in ages. "Not really. There's nothing more important than family. It's not like he's going to hurt you again. You've both changed."

He couldn't help the scoff that left his lips. "There's no guarantee of that." The mere suggestion that Samuel wouldn't interfere with his current relationship put Cameron on edge. He would never risk letting that happen. Until Sophia had a ring on her finger, she wouldn't be meeting his brother.

Cameron turned toward Sophia and forced a smile if only to distract her. "I don't think I was ever as close to my brother as you are with your siblings. There's been a good dose of rivalry between us even as kids. While he wouldn't let anyone pummel me or bully me, he didn't seem to mind —" He cut himself off before he said what was really in his heart.

His brother hadn't minded hurting him by flirting and ultimately stealing his girlfriend's affections. They hadn't even dated all that long.

Sophia reached out to his face and caressed him with her fingertips. "That's too bad. Because I'm sure it would be better if you had each other to lean on."

He grunted, but he wasn't going to give her the response she seemed to want. He and his brother had gotten back to being cordial, but they were far from close. Cameron figured their strained relationship would stay that way, and he had accepted it.

She snuggled in closer to him and rested her cheek against his chest. "One day you might find that it's worth mending the bridges that were torn apart between you. And when that time comes, I'll be there to hold your hand."

There was no fighting the smile that flooded his face. He would never tell her that he might consider doing just that if she swore to keep her end of the bargain. Something like that seemed to be too far into the future for him to worry about.

Cameron slipped his arm around her shoulders and pulled her closer. As long as he had her by his side, anything was possible.

As the weeks passed, Cameron continued to get more attached to Sophia. He was protective of her. He wanted what was best for her, and he wanted to be the one person who could be everything for her.

They spent almost every evening together, and he couldn't get enough of her. On the weekends, they'd run errands and sometimes hang out with her friends. Today was no different. They sat around a table at Sal's getting lunch, and Sophia laughed at something Emma said. It wasn't so bad spending time with Emma and her husband—mostly because Caleb clearly only had eyes for his wife.

Cameron didn't have to worry about Sophia being stolen away. As silly as that might sound to someone else, his fear was a tangible thing. Just the thought of her finding affection for someone else put his heart on edge.

"That's why I'm coming with her on her next trip. Can you believe they wanted to do a full international tour?" Caleb shook his head, but mirth still danced in his eyes.

Emma swatted at him. "Is that so hard to believe? I haven't been out of the country since the day we met."

Caleb dragged his blonde beauty into his side and pressed a kiss to her temple. "I'm more surprised that they haven't tried to do so sooner."

"Well, if you end up having a concert in Colorado again, I want to come. I'm always up for a fun night with music and dancing in some guy's arms." Sophia glanced at Cameron and winked, sending his heart into a flurry of emotion.

He wanted to believe that wink meant she was talking about him. But the fact that she said "some guy's arms" made his muscles tense. He wasn't just some guy. He was the guy who had fallen for her hard and fast.

Cameron's jaw set, but he managed to smile at her if only to ensure she didn't think she'd said anything to upset him. She was very aware of his struggles with jealousy and fear of losing her. He was working on it, but there were still moments that dragged him down.

As if she sensed his mood, she leaned into him.

"Hey, guys. Long time no see." Two men seemed to materialize at the table. Cameron didn't recognize either of them. They were both tall and tanned. Based on their builds, they probably worked with their hands out at one of the ranches that the town was known for.

One was blond, and the other had dark hair with some scruff lining his jaw. They both had brown eyes. By the way they let their focus trail over Sophia, it was clear they not only knew her but also liked her.

Fire burst in his chest and that fierce protective nature he had seemed to rear its ugly head. Under no circumstances would he let either one of them sit beside Sophia and—

"Hey, guys. Sit with us. We're just waiting for our food." Sophia patted the space beside her and scooted closer to Cameron. Caleb and Emma did the same. "Cameron, this is Trent and his brother Patrick. They work for Zeke Callahan. Guys, this is Cameron."

The two gave Cameron a nod, and he gave them a sharp one in return. He watched them with an intensity that even he wasn't prepared for. Trent was the blond one who sat next to Emma, and he was staring at Sophia like he wanted nothing more than to lean across the table and kiss the living daylights out of her.

Cameron's hands clenched into fists. This was how the whole thing with his brother had started. He was getting flashbacks of the night he'd taken Kristy to a casual diner like this one and his brother had shown up.

Samuel invited himself and a couple of his friends into the booth Cameron had picked, and the way he'd flirted with Kristy should have been the first indication that things would go downhill.

Couldn't Trent see that Sophia was here with someone? The way he was flashing his perfectly white smile seemed to indicate that even if he knew, he didn't care.

Sam hadn't cared either.

Sophia whirled to face him, her eyes widening slightly. "You okay?"

He stiffened. "What? Yeah, why?" All eyes were on him, and Sophia had started to blush somewhat. She glanced around the table, then back to Cameron. With everyone's attention on them, she wasn't going to tell him. And he wasn't willing to stick around and watch this Trent guy try to woo the girl Cameron loved so much. "Actually, we should go."

"But the food—"

"Now."

Sophia's blush intensified, and her eyes narrowed. "I want to stay, Cameron."

"And I want to go," he practically growled. Then he glanced around the table. "Sorry, guys, but we have something planned I forgot about."

"Cameron—" she started indignantly, but he waved at Patrick to get him to slide out of the booth so he could give Sophia a gentle push to follow.

By the time they had the waitress put their food in to-go cartons and he was guiding her out of the diner, Sophia was livid.

She spun to face him when they reached the side of his truck. "What was that for?"

He gritted his teeth.

"*Cameron.*" She folded her arms and stared daggers at

him. "Please tell me that this wasn't about your jealousy issues."

His eyes flicked to meet hers, and his anger wavered.

"It *was*, wasn't it?" Her hands fell to her sides, and she gaped at him. "You can't *do* stuff like that. Those guys are my friends. They probably think you're a total jerk now."

He frowned and glanced back at the diner. He *was* a jerk. The smallest sliver of remorse pained his midsection. "Sorry," he muttered.

"I mean it. You can't let your jealousy get the better of you. I have a lot of friends. I might not be super close to them, but I know a lot of people in town and... surprise, surprise, a lot of them are guys."

He let out a growl under his breath.

She whacked at him. "That. There it is again."

Cameron's brows lifted, and he stared at her with surprise. "What?"

"You made that sound when we were sitting in the booth. It was loud enough that everyone stopped and stared at you. I swear Trent thought you might shift into some kind of werewolf or something."

A smile tugged at his lips.

She whacked at him again. "It's not funny!"

In a flash of movement, he caught her hand and placed a kiss to the inside of her wrist. She heaved a sigh, and goosebumps trailed up her arms. "I need you to know that I'm not going anywhere. You can't keep living your life expecting that I'm going to just go traipsing off with the next guy who gives me a smile."

He shut his eyes and pulled her in closer. "I *know*," he groaned. "It's just... *hard*."

"Hey," she whispered, causing him to open his eyes. "I'm not going anywhere. Okay?"

"Okay," he said, though even as he said it, he knew she couldn't guarantee it. Sophia was a free spirit. One day she might realize just what she'd be stuck with if she stayed with him. And when that day came, he wasn't sure he'd be able to survive it.

19

———

Sophia

*E*ven though Cameron never asked her to, Sophia made a decision not to speak to the guys she was friends with whenever he was around—which was almost all the time lately. Her reasons were two-fold.

Sophia didn't want to trigger Cameron when he didn't have any reason to doubt her. It only made him feel worse about himself. The second reason was that she didn't want whoever it was to be in the line of fire if Cameron ended up doing something he regretted.

The fact of the matter was that he didn't completely trust her. How could he? Their relationship was built on their mutually flirtatious natures. In the beginning, he'd witnessed just how easy it was for her to draw in any guy she was interested in.

On top of her needing to find a way to show him she was here for the long haul, he was dealing with his own unresolved issues with his brother. She didn't know Cameron's brother, but she got the distinct feeling that it would be good for them both to hash out what had happened. It didn't matter that Cameron had said they worked through their stuff. Clearly, he was still rattled enough that seeing any guy talk to Sophia triggered those latent fears.

She heaved a sigh as she settled back on the couch in her living room. Cameron had to go to an auction in the next town over. He'd gone with Mateo, and the two of them had invited her to tag along, but she couldn't manage it.

Trying to maintain the peace with Cameron had gotten exhausting. They had been dating for a couple of months now, and she still didn't feel he was any closer to being healed. Maybe he needed to see someone. There could be more to his issues than just the betrayal his brother had caused him.

"Everything okay?" Roman wandered into the living room with a cup of coffee in his hand. It was lunchtime.

She eyed the mug, her lip curling with a smidge of judgment. "How many cups of coffee have you had so far today?"

Her brother shrugged. "I don't count anymore."

Sophia snickered. "The fact that you can sleep at all at night still baffles me."

He took another sip. "What's going on? You don't have your usual shadow with you."

She huffed and wrapped her arms around her head. "Don't call him that." Just because she could tell that something was off about the way Cameron treated her didn't mean she wanted anyone else to point it out to her.

"What? He is. And I feel like it's getting worse."

Her arms fell to her sides. "You do?"

Roman gave her a flat look. "Honestly, I was skeptical

about him in the beginning, but I thought that maybe it was just because of the relationship being new. There were times when he was really good to you, too. But…"

"But?" she prodded.

He lifted one shoulder in a shrug. "Doesn't he seem a little too… I dunno… He's not controlling, is he?"

Her brows lifted. "Of course not." At the look her brother gave her, she sighed. "Really. He's not controlling at all. He just has some issues that we need to work through."

"Issues?"

It was her turn to shrug. She didn't like speaking about this with her brother. He could go tell Mateo the second he heard that something wrong was going on. Then Mateo would have to sit down with the two of them and work out whatever this was. Sophia sighed again. "He's *not* controlling. I can promise you that. He's just a little mistrusting."

"He doesn't trust you?" Roman said, a hint of anger in his voice.

"Not me… I don't think. Honestly, I think he trusts me. It's the other guys he doesn't trust."

"Other guys?" Roman frowned this time. "You're not…"

She blushed a deep red color. "No. I'm not cheating if that is what you're insinuating. And I'm not comfortable giving you his life story. Let's just say that he has some legitimate reasons to be worried that another guy will sweep me off my feet and he'll lose me."

Roman's frown only deepened. "I don't know if you should still be seeing this guy."

"What?" Sophia snapped. "Why not?"

"Because he's not ready for something serious."

She scoffed. "What do you know?"

He shrugged before taking another swig of his coffee.

"Love can do a lot to overcome things, but if someone has some deep-seated issues they haven't processed, then they should fix them before trying to bring someone else into their life."

Sophia chewed on her fingernail as she considered what her brother was saying. It made sense. Wasn't that the reason that she'd refused to date anyone for the last several years? She knew she wasn't ready for anything serious—not until she'd met Cameron. She'd needed to heal herself, and that had taken time.

Cameron hadn't done that yet.

She let out a groan. What was she supposed to do if he wasn't going to do what it took to get over this? She couldn't keep living her life avoiding anyone of the male persuasion.

"You know I'm right," Roman said.

"Yeah, well, doesn't mean I'm happy about it." She stared hard at her brother. "Things are going great between us. He hasn't had a jealous outburst in a long time. I can tell he's really trying." Especially when she ended up having to speak to some guy who happened to be one of Mateo's vendors for the ranch.

"All I'm saying is that you really should think about this before you let things go too far. Cameron is a decent guy. I'm not saying he isn't. But there are just some parts of our souls that should go through the healing process before we finally give it to the person we love."

Ugh. She hated that he was right. But how was she going to bring it up to him? Cameron would probably think she was breaking up with him instead of insisting that he work on himself.

A sigh built in her chest.

"If you need help talking to him—"

"It's *fine*," Sophia said. "I'll figure it out."

THE MUSIC in the country club wasn't enough to distract Sophia from what she knew she needed to bring up with Cameron. She was terrified about how he would react, and she couldn't find the words she needed to say to get him to understand she still didn't plan on going anywhere.

Sophia downed the water bottle that she'd gotten a few minutes ago, much to Cameron's amusement.

"Easy, tiger. You're going to get a stomachache."

"Too late for that," she said.

Cameron frowned. "Everything okay?"

Her eyes darted to anywhere in the building but him. This was a difficult conversation, and she wasn't sure having it here would be the best idea, but having it at the house wasn't a good option either. The last thing she needed was for her brothers to overhear any of it.

She cleared her throat and shook her head.

"What do you need?" His voice was immediately concerned, and it made her feel loved and wanted all at once.

Sophia lifted the empty bottle. "Do you think you could go get me another one? I think I'm just dehydrated."

He nodded. "I'll be right back." Cameron moved through the building toward the counter where they sold beverages, and she watched him until he disappeared into the crowd. Maybe talking to him at home would be best after all.

If she said the wrong thing here, then they'd have the most miserable car ride home.

"Is that Sophia, I see?"

She stiffened and glanced in the direction the voice had come from. Then her stomach dropped. "Brent?" Her hands curled into fists at her sides, though she fought to have her expression remain neutral. It had been nearly a decade since he'd cheated on her. Nearly a decade since she'd had to see him face to face. He'd left town, and she'd thought that was the end of it.

"In the flesh." Brent pulled her in for a hug, but before she could shove him away from her, he was yanked backward by the collar of his shirt.

Her eyes flew to the cause, and then they widened when she took in the anger emanating from Cameron's face. The way he looked at her was as if he believed she'd been the one to instigate this situation. He was hurting, but he was covering it up with an anger so hot that even Brent looked worried.

"Look, man, I don't know who you are—"

"Keep your hands off of my girl."

His girl? The way he said it made her sound more like property than an actual girlfriend. And while there was some small part of her that wouldn't mind seeing Brent roughed up a little for what he'd done to her, the more reasonable side of her knew this wasn't right.

"Cameron," she snapped, but he didn't look at her. He was still glaring at Brent like he was planning on sending him to his maker for trying to hug her.

He shifted so he stood between Sophia and Brent, and then he gave the guy a measurable shove against the chest. Brent stumbled back a step, and his foot caught on something, sending him sprawling to the ground.

The fight caught the attention of several people nearby,

and Sophia fought the embarrassment flooding her face when their eyes turned to her with curiosity.

"Cameron!" she attempted again, but he was standing over Brent, his stance daring the guy to get to his feet.

Still, people gasped and murmured as Brent garbled out some nonsense and Cameron continued to lay claim to her like she wasn't anything more than an object.

She let out a strangled sound and shoved past Cameron to the door. She could feel his attention before she heard his voice. "Sophia!"

The crowd parted for her as she made her way to the exit, phone in hand. She had an Uber ordered before she made it to the bottom steps of the country club. And they were only two minutes out by the time Cameron stood beside her.

He touched her arm, and she yanked it away.

"Red," he whispered, "you have to understand—"

She whirled on him. "I don't have to understand anything, Cameron. What you did in there wasn't appropriate. You should have never laid your hands on him, no matter who he was."

"Who he was? You *know* him." It wasn't a question, more like an accusation.

Sophia huffed, pulling her eyes from him to stare at her phone.

"What are you doing?" He made to reach for her phone, and she dodged his attempt.

"I'm getting a ride."

"I'm your ride."

"Not tonight, you aren't."

"Sophia," he tried again, but she held up a hand to stop him.

"We're not going to talk about this here. All I'm going to say is that you promised you wouldn't make a scene like that. You promised," she said, her voice cracking.

"I know," he said, his shoulders sagging. Before he could say anything else, a car pulled up and a girl rolled down the window to look at them.

"Sophia?"

Nodding, Sophia moved to the car, but Cameron stopped her.

"Please, can we—"

"Later, Cameron."

"Sophia, I..."

She paused with her hand on the door.

He swallowed hard. "You've done a number on me, Sophia. You're my reason for living."

Her expression softened, and as much as she wanted to accept his confession of his feelings for what it was, she knew it wasn't enough. They would still need to discuss how to fix this. They just couldn't do it here, and she was too exhausted to do it tonight. "We'll talk about this later." With that, she climbed into the car and the driver pulled away.

20

Cameron

Guilt ate at Cameron worse than ever before. He couldn't believe what he'd done last night in front of everyone. He still didn't know what that guy meant to Sophia, and since she didn't seem interested in telling him, he wasn't sure he ever would.

All he knew was that she had hit her breaking point, and he wasn't sure he knew how to come back from it.

There was one glaring issue with his guilt, however.

He didn't regret laying his claim on Sophia in the slightest. The crowd that had surrounded them as he tore into that guy who sniveled on the floor meant that everyone who was in attendance knew that Sophia belonged to him. They were an item.

Well, they were.

She hadn't exactly broken up with him, and part of him wondered if that was what she wanted to talk about.

No. He couldn't think that way. He needed to believe that she cared for him as much as she said she did. How could she put up with him this far and not?

He had the hardest time focusing on his work, and it was made even worse by the fact that Sophia hadn't shown up to do her usual work. He lost track of how many times he'd nearly gone in search of her or asked some of the men if they'd seen her.

Heck, he'd almost asked Roman, but based on the less-than-pleased look the guy gave him, Cameron thought better of it.

The horses were doing well. The pregnancies were coming along as expected, and their bloodwork came back normal.

Mateo checked in periodically, but it was Sophia who usually got the full report. At the thought of her, he glanced over his shoulder, expecting to see her crossing over from the house toward the barn. But she wasn't there.

He frowned.

There had to be something he could do to show her how sorry he was. He needed her to know he loved her. But what could he do?

Words seemed trite at this point. He'd lost track of how many times he'd told her that he was working on improving himself and that he'd do better.

She'd been right. He'd made a promise at that diner that day, and he'd broken it.

His heart sagged in his chest the more he dwelled on his problems. Doing nothing would be worse than biting the bullet and making a fool of himself in whatever way he could come up with.

After his work was done, he found himself in town at a

floral shop. Flowers didn't feel like they would be enough, but they'd be a start. He picked out a card, too. It had a cartoon night sky on the front, and inside, it had some silly note about the object of his affection being brighter than all the stars in the night sky.

It reminded him of the night they'd spent cuddled together talking about what was important in life. He traced a finger over the image for a moment, then placed it on the counter and picked up a pen as the florist put the flowers into a vase.

He'd make this right. Nothing could be worse than what had happened at the country club. Cameron had hit rock bottom, and there was nowhere left to go but up.

Cameron paid for the flowers, then gathered them into his arms and headed home. He knocked on her door, but when no one answered, he situated himself on the porch and waited. That was the hardest part. He hadn't thought anything could have been worse than the way she'd looked at him last night, but waiting to see her again in the flesh was utterly terrifying. What if she still didn't want to see him?

What if she wanted to break things off?

He couldn't think that way or he wouldn't be able to continue waiting for her.

Time lost all meaning as he sat there, stewing over what he'd done. The side of him that believed he'd been in the right warred with the one that wanted to make Sophia happy. The only way to ensure that no one would try that again would be to put a ring on her finger, right?

She wouldn't accept his proposal right now, though. And part of him couldn't help but wonder if that wasn't the solution at all as much as he wanted it.

Cameron heaved a sigh, and his head snapped up when he saw her car come closer to the house. Once parked, three doors opened and Sophia stepped out with her two sisters. Her eyes snagged on him for a moment, and then she glanced at her siblings briefly before nodding to them.

Isabelle and Camilla gave her reassuring smiles before they gathered their bags from the car and headed into the house.

He moved down the steps, the flowers in his hand. "Hey," he murmured when they were alone.

"Hey," she whispered back. Sophia couldn't have been more guarded than she was at this moment. He could practically see the walls she'd erected since the last time they'd seen one another.

How was he going to make this better?

Her eyes dipped to the flowers in his hand, and he followed her attention. Then without missing a beat, he pushed them toward her. "These are for you."

Sophia continued to stare at them, gnawing on her lower lip. For a heartrending moment, he thought she might refuse his offer. Just when he'd nearly given up hope, she reached for them. Her fingers brushed against his, and she whispered, "Thank you."

Cameron shoved his hands into his pockets. He'd never considered himself the type of person who struggled with his relationships. He'd never had to deal with the sort of raging jealousies that came with caring for Sophia. Even when his brother had betrayed him by stealing his girlfriend's affection, his temper hadn't been this hard to contain.

That was either a good thing or a very bad thing.

She didn't look up at him, choosing instead to stare at the flowers in her hand. The only thing he wanted was to turn back time. If he could go back to before he'd made a fool of himself, he would. But there was no changing the past. He was at risk of losing her completely if he couldn't pull himself together.

"I'm sorry," he mumbled.

Her eyes lifted.

"I'm really sorry, Sophia."

She swallowed audibly and shifted her weight from one foot to the other. "I feel like I've heard that before."

He flinched, his gut tightening uncomfortably. This wasn't going to be as simple as an apology, and he knew it.

"I've really been trying to be patient." Her words were barely above a whisper. "I've tried to make sure that I'm not contributing to your... issues."

He grimaced again, and he hated how her words stung him. She wasn't wrong. He had issues. There was no denying them. He ignored the self-deprecating feeling that came along with that acknowledgment. Heat flared to life beneath his skin, and he couldn't help lifting his hand to rub at the back of his neck. "I never wanted you to—"

"Let me finish." She pierced him with a pleading gaze.

Cameron nodded sharply.

She breathed out a sigh. "I get it, Cameron. With what happened with your brother, I can understand your concerns about losing someone you care for."

Why did her statement not bring him the comfort he wanted it to?

"But it's exhausting."

The statement he'd started returned to the tip of his lips.

He didn't want to put this on her. The fact that he had only made the guilt worse. "I'll do better." Would she only hear an empty promise?

She frowned.

"I know I said that before. The problem isn't with the guys who hang around you. It's... with me." He blew out a heavy breath and dropped his hand to his side. "And my brother."

She opened her mouth as if she were going to reject his claim, but he pushed forward.

"To expect a stranger to have the same tendencies as my brother had when we were younger isn't fair to anyone involved."

Sophia's brows pulled together. Apparently, she'd changed her mind about speaking whatever it was that she'd nearly said.

He stepped closer to her and took her hand in his own. His thumb traced circles on the back of her hand, and he stared hard at the movement as he considered his next words carefully. "If I'm completely honest, I don't regret what I did—not entirely."

She tugged to remove her hand from his, but he held fast.

"Sophia," he said, his heart hammering in his chest. "I feel bad about how I treated the guy... but I don't feel bad showing people how much I care about you. We belong together." He closed the remaining distance between them, pulling her to him by the nape of her neck before he pressed his forehead against hers. "You belong to me."

The way her body tensed at his words gave him pause. They were probably not the best words to say at this moment, but at least she didn't argue with him. That had to be a good sign, right?

He drew in a shuddering breath and closed his eyes, reveling in the way she smelled, in the way she felt beside him. Then he opened his eyes and set them on her with a confidence he didn't feel at all in his core. "I know that I've made mistakes, Red. More than I can count. But there is something drawing me to you that I have never been able to shake. Over the last five years, I compared any woman who wanted to get close to me... I compared them to *you*."

Her soft gasp gave him an ounce of courage to continue.

"The bar was high, and I'm not entirely convinced any of them could have come close." He searched her eyes, unsure of what he was looking for. She seemed stunned. Gone was the anxiety, though. And it almost felt like her walls were cracking. All she needed was one little shove in the right direction. "I love you, Red," he whispered huskily.

Then he leaned down and brushed a feather-light kiss to her full lips. The only solace he had was the fact that she didn't pull away. She didn't push him back or hurl insults at him.

But what hurt the most was her utter lack of a returning confession.

He withdrew just enough to look her in the eyes, and all he saw were warring emotions. It was understandable. She didn't have to return his sentiments with a confession of her own. That would happen in time.

At least, he prayed it would.

Cameron took a step back, dropping the hand he still held. "Goodnight, Sophia." With that, he turned away from her and headed to his truck. He couldn't stick around in case she chose to officially break things off with him. His heart wouldn't be able to handle such a rejection, not after he'd left his heart in her hands to do with as she pleased.

If this experience taught him anything, it was that he needed to focus on controlling his temper. There was too much at risk, and he wasn't about to lose her over something as dumb as his jealousy.

21

Sophia

"**A**rgh. Why does he have to be so charming?" Sophia placed her face in her hands. "Am I crazy?"

Emma swirled her straw in her drink as she sat across from Sophia in a booth at Sal's. One side of her mouth quirked upward, and she let out a chuckle. "What part are you asking about?"

Sophia gave her a flat look—one that probably gave away the fact that she was somewhat confused.

Once again, Emma laughed. "Meaning, are you crazy because his behavior bothers you? Or are you crazy because it doesn't bother you enough?"

Another groan spilled from Sophia's lips, and she shook her head. "Both."

Emma shrugged. "Don't you have your own sort of jealousy issues? I recall that you used your flirtatious behavior to get back at that guy when he first moved here."

She covered her flushed face with her hands again. "Don't remind me."

"I don't know," Emma hedged. "I can see both sides."

Upon Sophia's confused look, Emma sighed.

"Honestly, it's nice to know that he doesn't want you to give your attention to anyone else. It shows how much he cares about you—"

"Narcissists behave the same way, you know," Sophia interrupted. "It's the whole 'if I can't have her then no one can' mentality."

Emma rolled her eyes. "And do you think that Cameron fits that profile?"

Sophia hunched back into her seat with a sigh. She picked at the fries on her plate. "No. I think he's got past scars that make it difficult for him to deal with the idea of losing me."

"That's my point. He might be obsessive, and while that can feel suffocating, it can also be reassuring in a... different kind of way."

"I sense a 'but' coming," Sophia hedged.

"But..." Emma drawled. "It's not healthy when it interferes with your relationship. If it's changing your personality and you can't hang out with friends... if it puts you on edge and stresses you out... then maybe he's not right for you."

A pit opened up in her stomach like a black hole. Sophia didn't like the sound of that at all. When Cameron had told her he loved her, she'd been so thrown off that she hadn't responded. It had been a couple days, and they hadn't spoken of that moment—or anything intimate, for that matter. He was giving her space, and she had appreciated it. Now, she was missing him like a phantom limb. "You think we should break up."

"I won't say it's not... *concerning*." That said it all. Emma had noticed, and she was worried.

Sophia chewed on her lower lip, wondering if she could actually walk away from him. They'd shared so much with each other that she felt like doing so would break her more than what Brent had done.

Emma's hand wrapped around hers, drawing her attention. "All I'm saying is that you need to have a long conversation about this. There needs to be ground rules—clear expectations. And maybe it wouldn't hurt for Cameron to see a therapist. Honey, you could see one too."

At that suggestion, Sophia balked.

Emma held up both hands. "Don't shoot the messenger. Seriously, we all have traumas that we don't heal from fully. Everyone could use a good meeting with someone who knows how to listen and point out the obvious."

Sophia snorted. "Yeah, maybe you're right."

"I know I'm right." Emma grinned at her. "But to answer your question. No. I don't think you need to break up with him. Has he made mistakes? Sure. But has any harm been done?" She shrugged again. "I mean, he hasn't actually beaten anyone up, right? For me? That'd be the line he couldn't cross. So, I guess you just have to decide where that line is for you."

Drinking in her suggestions, Sophia allowed her thoughts to wander. Emma was right. Cameron hadn't really hurt anyone. He wasn't controlling her—preventing her from leaving her home or spending time with friends. He was just... overprotective.

Geez, now it sounded like she was making excuses.

The best bit of advice Emma had given her was that bit about the therapist. Cameron could use something like that. He hadn't gotten over what had happened with his brother. And if what her gut was telling her was correct, then Cameron would consider doing just that if only to ensure their relationship continued to strengthen. She gave Emma a nod. "I like the way you think. I'll talk with him tonight."

Sophia ran a few more errands in town after her meeting with Emma. She wasn't sure if she was delaying the inevitable when she decided to grab an ice cream and eat it in the park. Bringing up therapy with Cameron had to be done with care. She couldn't imagine anyone would want to be cornered and told that they needed help.

She released a heavy breath, one that felt like she'd been holding since her coffee date with Emma. But then that air got caught in her throat as her eyes locked with a pair of familiar blues.

He was dressed casually, and he held a bag from the local bookstore in his hand. A slow smile stretched on his lips as they continued to stare at each other from about ten feet away. "Sophia, as I live and breathe."

Heat immediately flooded her face, and she glanced away as if she could escape. It had been four years since she'd seen Sam. She'd met him the summer after that debacle with Cameron, and they'd hit it off—well, as much as she could with any guy. He was the only other man who convinced her to go on additional dates, though they didn't call them that.

Hangout sessions. No pressure for anything more. He lived in the city, and she was here. Sam would come to

Copper Creek just to spend the weekend with her, and she'd kept him a complete secret from her siblings.

Shoot. He was coming right for her.

She cleared her throat, making sure she hadn't lost her voice, even though at this moment it certainly felt like she had. "What are you doing in town?"

His smile broadened, and the natural charisma the man had seemed to melt some of the anxiety swirling within her. Why she felt that anxiety, she couldn't be certain. She didn't still have feelings for him. In fact, compared to how she felt about Cameron, they were non-existent. If anything, she'd continued to spend time with him because he was familiar—comforting.

Sam took a seat beside her on the bench and, without a word, reached for her cone.

She gasped indignantly when he took a decisive lick of her treat. "Hey!"

He chuckled and leaned back on the bench, his legs sprawled out. "I'm visiting family."

"Family?" She wracked her brain. "I didn't think you had any family in town."

With a shake of his head, he let out a sigh. "I didn't. But apparently now I do."

Sophia studied him. *Apparently.* Whatever that meant.

His eyes swept over to her once more. He wasn't shy with the way his gaze raked over her body with appreciation. "You're looking as good as ever."

With a roll of her eyes, she settled back against the bench and took another lick of her ice cream. "Looks like you haven't changed at all. Empty compliments meant to get me to swoon for you?" She hid a smile behind her ice cream.

That was another reason why they'd never worked out. They were just too similar.

Sophia had expected him to laugh and toss a teasing statement to her, but when he didn't, her happy expression faltered and she stared at him again. He looked utterly serious.

"What?"

Sam sat upright and turned to face her, a contemplative look replacing the easy smile he'd worn upon approach. "Do you really think that?" Was there pain in his voice? Or was she imagining it?

Her ice cream forgotten, Sophia stared at him right back. "What?"

"Do you really think that I gave you empty compliments?"

She forced a laugh, not liking the tension that had suddenly wrapped around them. The way they'd ended things had been clean. He'd wanted more than she did, but they were both happy to go their separate ways.

But looking at him now, she couldn't help but wonder if he'd been pretending. "Well," she swallowed hard, "that was just the way we were with each other."

His frown deepened. "I never said anything I didn't mean, Sophia."

A confession that should have given her goosebumps did nothing but put her on edge. Guilt slipped past her defenses, and she suddenly didn't feel hungry enough to finish her treat. "Yeah, okay. But you can't tell me that you were being serious when you said we were fated to be together." She said it flippantly. It was the only thing that popped into her mind from their interactions. "I mean, you were always sweet, and you made me feel special, but—"

He placed a hand on her knee, cutting her off, and she glanced down at the touch. His warm hand was a stark contrast to her cool skin, and she couldn't drag her attention away until his words ripped her to the present.

"Sophia, I was in love with you."

Her head snapped up and she flushed hot and cold all at once—not because she'd felt anything for him then or even now. She was embarrassed she'd blinded herself to the fact that his feelings ran deeper.

She choked out a laugh as if that motion alone would be enough to shatter the weight that was suddenly pressing down on her. When he didn't even do her the decency of cracking a smile, she stilled. "You were not." Her voice was flat, void of emotion. And yet it almost felt like she was pleading with him to admit that she was right.

Sam lifted a hand and ran it through his hair with a heavy sigh. "I was." He peered up at the sky and a ghost of a smile touched his lips. He didn't meet her gaze when he continued. "You were the one who got away, Sophia. You were the girl I thought I might marry one day."

She blinked several times, her head feeling dizzy. "But we were friends."

This time he gave her a wry smile. "Yeah, we were."

Then she poked him in the chest, her frustration edging her voice. "You said that it would be best if you stopped coming around."

He shrugged. "What can I say? It was torture to be around you, knowing you didn't feel the same." His eyes flicked to hers several times, and if she wasn't mistaken, she thought she could see coloring flood his cheeks. Was he embarrassed? "I don't suppose anything has changed? Seeing me hasn't sparked something in you?"

When she couldn't find the words to say anything, he barked a laugh.

"No, I didn't suppose it would." He heaved another heavy sigh as he got to his feet, and as if against her will, she followed suit.

"I'm so sorry, Sam. I didn't know."

He cocked his head, his eyes delving into hers for longer than they should. "Nah, I think you did. I just think you weren't ready. Or maybe you were, but your heart belonged to someone else."

Her heart thundered at his words.

Cameron.

Maybe he was right. Over the last five years, she'd still thought about the guy who had managed to break her heart in less than a week.

He pulled her in for a hug and instinctively, she hugged him back. "It was nice seeing you, Sophia. Maybe we can hang out later this weekend?"

They started to pull away from one another, and she turned to tell him that might not be a good idea just as he moved to kiss her cheek.

The result was an awkward smooch that could only be described as what it felt like to kiss her grandmother. Before she knew what was happening, a blur of color tackled Sam to the ground.

22

———

Cameron

*B*linding rage.

That was the only emotion that built behind Cameron's eyes as he took swing after swing at his brother. He lost track of how many times he pummeled his own flesh and blood before strong hands dragged him off Samuel.

Only then did he register that Sophia was screaming at him.

Someone was calling the sheriff.

Several people were watching him as his chest rose and fell with sharp breaths. His lungs burned, but the pain in his knuckles was even worse. Samuel looked disoriented as someone helped him to his feet. He glowered at Cameron.

He wiped at the blood that dribbled from his nose and split lip. He mumbled a curse under his breath. "Cameron? Are you insane?"

Hands tightened on his arm, and Cameron yanked free,

only to realize that it was Sophia's touch that he pulled away from. She froze. Her eyes darted from Cameron to Samuel and back again.

"You guys know each other?"

Samuel seemed just as confused, but not Cameron. Somehow, he knew something like this would happen. Sam spat blood on the grass before jerking his chin at Cameron. "He's my brother."

Sophia gasped and looked to Cameron for confirmation. "What?"

Shaking out his hands, Cameron shook his head. "I don't have a brother." He expected to see a reaction from Samuel or even Sophia, but no one moved. They were in a stand-off. He lost track of the seconds that ticked by as he tried to make heads or tails of how this catastrophe had occurred.

Then he whirled around and faced the love of his life. She'd kissed another man—his brother, no less. Every fear Cameron had was manifested in the moments leading up to what he'd witnessed.

He'd come to town to meet with his brother. They were going to get lunch and catch up, and Cameron had been stupid enough to think if he kept Samuel contained in the city, there wouldn't be any chance of Sophia running into him.

But he hadn't counted on the fact that Sophia was going to be in town as well.

At first, he'd sat back and watched the interaction. Cameron knew his brother. He knew that Samuel wouldn't pass up a chance to flirt with a girl as pretty as Sophia. She was his type, as history had shown. Cameron hadn't been surprised in the slightest to see Samuel take a seat to joke around with Sophia.

Maybe it was morbid curiosity, but Cameron had been more interested to see what Sophia would do when a stranger hit on her without him present.

His fingernails had dug into his hands the longer he'd watched them. He'd been so proud of himself for holding back when he saw Samuel move closer to speak to her. Every memory of seeing Samuel with his ex had been yanked to the surface while Cameron watched the interaction, and he just prayed that Samuel would get up and walk away.

Alas, his prayers had gone unanswered.

"You kissed him," he growled at Sophia. "You kissed my brother."

"What?" Her eyes widened. "No, I didn't."

"I saw it with my own eyes." He let out a mirthless laugh that sounded almost sinister. "You can't tell me I was seeing things because I know what I saw." His heart was shattering and all the pain from his past came rushing to the surface. "The worst part is that you know how it would make me feel."

This was personal.

Sophia reached for him, shaking her head. Cameron ignored the way the crowd hovered as if they wanted to listen to the gossip that would assuredly be spread like dandelion seeds by the end of the day. Her eyes pricked with emotion. "Cameron, whatever you think happened—"

"I *know* what happened," he snapped.

"Cam, just wait—" Samuel started.

Cameron shot him a death glare. "You stay out of this. Haven't you done enough?"

His brother took a step closer. "It's not what you think, Cam. She's telling the truth."

Another laugh bubbled from Cameron's throat. It

burned like acid coming up, and he shook his head before lacing his fingers behind his neck and taking a few paces. "It's not what I think. Yeah, where have I heard that before? Oh, right. That first time I caught you with Kristy."

Samuel had the decency to snap his mouth shut. His skin colored in a strange blotchy kind of way. "What can I say? She wasn't content with what she had." He said it with all the smugness of a man who knew he could get any girl to fall at his feet.

Cameron lunged for his brother, ready to take another swing, but Sophia's strangled voice stopped him. She moved toward Cameron, blocking him from having a direct path to his brother. Her dark eyes pierced him. "You can't just throw punches anytime you don't like what someone says."

He scoffed.

"I mean it, Cameron. It's not healthy."

"You want to talk about healthy? How about we talk about your incessant need to use your flirting like a bonafide weapon?"

Sophia gasped.

Samuel muttered under his breath but had the intelligence to keep those thoughts to himself.

Cameron stepped into her, his eyes narrowing on her. "You use your so-called skills to benefit you. Why can't I use my fists to benefit me?"

"Cameron!" she admonished.

"How am I supposed to believe you're telling the truth when I know how your mind works, hmm? From the looks of it, the two of you were laughing and having a good time. Let me ask you something, Red. Did you tell him you were involved with anyone?" His eyes darted from her to Samuel. The latter couldn't control the surprise on his face. His brother was usually very good at schooling his features, but he was utterly floored. A sneer stretched Cameron's face. "She didn't, did she?" He directed that question at his brother. "We are dating. Which begs the question. Why not? Why didn't you tell *Sam* that you were involved? You certainly had plenty of time."

Guilt permeated her expression, and for some unexplainable reason, seeing it hit him harder than witnessing the bumbling kiss from a few minutes ago. She placed her hands on his chest, her eyes pleading. "I swear I didn't know Sam was your brother."

Hollow.

Her words did nothing to fill the void he was feeling as he stood there staring at her while she attempted to make him feel better. She *knew* how this would affect him—what it would do to him for her to be involved with his brother. Not only that, but his trust continued to crumble knowing she hadn't said a single word about her relationship status.

"We met four years ago," she stammered. Still, that confession did nothing to ease the ache in his chest.

Vague memories of Samuel flooded his mind. His mother had said that Samuel had met a girl he was interested in, but then nothing had come of it. Was that woman Sophia?

His focus bounced from Samuel to Sophia. Of course it was her. Who wouldn't fall for her charm and her wit? He'd fallen for her in less than twenty-four hours. Why wouldn't his brother do the same?

A sick, twisted feeling was brought to life again, and he pried Sophia's hands from his chest. His grip on her wrists was firm but not enough to be painful. The hurt in her eyes gave him a momentary pause. He was torn between wanting to push her away for her deception—planned or not—and wanting to pull her close so they could heal together.

Cameron dropped her hands and stepped back. His voice was gravelly and full of anguish. "You know what? Have him. You two deserve each other." He spun on his heel but was stopped by the sheriff arriving.

Twenty minutes later and with an insistence that Samuel wasn't going to press charges, Cameron was permitted to escape to his truck. He didn't get far, however. He heard her footsteps before she appeared at his side.

Her breaths came out heavy, and her cheeks were stained with dried tears. "Cameron, we need to talk."

He huffed. "There's nothing to talk about."

"Yes, there is."

Cameron shook his head. "You've made it perfectly clear that you don't want to lay claim on me. My brother. Your ex. Some random guy at that country club. Doesn't matter. It was inevitable."

She made a strangled sound that had his steps faltering. He glanced in her direction to see a fresh wave of tears. But this time they weren't full of sadness. Those were angry tears. Her hands were balled into fists, and if she was anyone else, she might have taken a swing at him. "Will you just stop for a minute?"

He did as she asked and faced her, though he couldn't look directly into her eyes. His focus remained on a blank space to the right of her head. "What?" he snapped. She didn't speak right away, and for a moment he considered making his escape. This whole thing was a total mess. He'd ruined everything with his outburst. Even now, there were bits of clarity coming through as guilt and shame accosted him. His eyes flickered to her face, and the look of desperation he read there was like a kick to the groin. Cameron hefted out a sigh and ran a hand through his hair. "What?"

She blinked furious tears, her fingers now twitching at her sides. Then she folded her arms across her chest. "You need help."

He nearly stumbled back a step. "What?"

"You heard me. Something is going on, and it's nothing I can help you with. You should get professional help before you really do some damage. Do you know how lucky you are that Samuel is your brother?"

"Lucky?" he scoffed with a derisive laugh. "You and I have very different views on what that word means."

She flushed a deep, angry, scarlet color. "I mean it, Cameron. If that had been a stranger, you might have been put in lockup. I'm not even entirely sure the sheriff won't do it just to make an example out of you."

Cameron's eyes darted to the group of people who were too far away to hear their conversation. The sheriff was still speaking to a few of the witnesses. Stomach lurching, Cameron brought his focus once more to Sophia.

"Will you say something?" she asked, meeker this time.

"What do you want me to say?" he asked, emotionless. "You want me to thank my brother for kissing the only girl I could think about for the last five years?"

She blinked rapidly.

"You want me to beg forgiveness from you when I did nothing wrong? I'm certainly not the one keeping my relationship a secret. That's all on you, Red."

He could see in real time her fury returning.

"You know what?" she snapped. "Fine. Do what you want. But until something changes, don't bother speaking to me." With that, she spun around and charged back to the crowd of people.

He groaned, yanking at his hair. "Sophia, wait—"

But she didn't. She just kept walking.

Back to her bench, to the sheriff, to the place where his world had turned upside down.

And back to Sam.

23

Sophia

Sophia had insisted she was fine when Sam offered to walk her to her truck. She'd insisted he leave her alone when he'd asked if he could call her tomorrow. And she'd insisted that she still didn't have any feelings for him when he gave her those puppy dog eyes that were only part of the problem she currently faced.

Sam looked nothing like his brother. One must have taken after their mother while the other took after their father. They were both flirtatious in their own rights and charming as all get-out.

Maybe that was why she'd been drawn to Sam four years ago. There was something familiar about the way Sam was.

The tears had stopped falling long ago, but her pillowcase was still saturated with them. Today couldn't have gone worse if she'd tried to make it so. She'd wanted to sit down with Cameron and tell him how proud she was about the changes he was trying to make before she brought up the idea of therapy.

She'd wanted to assure him she'd be with him every step of the way.

Most of all, she hadn't wanted to walk away from him without looking back.

Her chest ached. Her eyes burned. And based on the way her mouth felt, she could have spent the last week in the middle of the desert.

The things he'd said to her resonated in her chest and bounced around painfully in her head. While she didn't regret what she'd said to him, she did regret one thing.

It would have been smart to tell Sam about Cameron right from the start. There really hadn't been any excuse. He'd brought up dating life. She could have easily told him that she'd found someone to fall in love with.

Why hadn't she?

The question haunted her. She cared for Cameron. More than that, she loved him. She knew as much based on the empty feeling where her heart should be. And yet, she still struggled to commit to him in the way most healthy individuals did. Most people shouted it from the rooftops when they found the person they wanted to spend the rest of their life with.

Did that mean she didn't want that?

Had she been alone for so long that she'd forgotten what it felt like to *want* that in her life?

Perhaps.

Maybe she still wasn't ready to commit to someone.

Sophia shut her eyes tight, hating how selfish it felt to be... *her*.

Emma was right. It wasn't just the people who had anger

issues who needed therapy. Something was wrong with her, and deep down she wasn't sure she wanted to fix it. That thought terrified her for no other reason than the fact that she'd have to look Cameron in the eyes and tell him that she still needed him.

A soft knock sounded at her bedroom door before it opened. Roman's head popped inside, and he stared at her with concern. "Someone's here to see you."

"No," she muttered.

"But you don't know who—"

"I know exactly who it is, and I don't want to see him."

Roman withdrew for a moment, then entered the room and shut the door behind him. He leaned against it with folded arms, his frown deepening. "As much as I want to play the overprotective brother right now, I feel it's my duty to tell you that Cameron seems legitimately sorry."

She scoffed and turned her back to him, facing the other wall instead. "Where have I heard that before?"

His footsteps shuffled along her plush carpet, then the mattress dipped, and he sighed. "It's not just that he's sorry. I'm worried about you. Even if you don't want to resolve this with him, you need closure. And then there's Mateo to think about."

She scowled. "Yeah. I bet Mateo is *thrilled* this turned out exactly how he predicted. Let me guess. You've had to hold him back so he didn't march in here and tell me I'm irresponsible and now I'm disowned or something."

There was silence for a moment. Longer than a moment. She turned over and glanced at him over her shoulder just to see if Roman was still there.

Her brother wasn't looking at her. He was staring at a spot on the wall, his brows furrowed.

"Roman?"

Slowly, he turned his attention to her. "He isn't going to leave until you speak to him."

"He will if you give him the same courtesy he gave his brother yesterday."

The mere fact that Roman didn't look confused or surprised by her statement made it perfectly clear that he was aware of what had transpired in town yesterday. Her scowl deepened, and she folded her arms as she stared up at her ceiling. They remained like that, in silence for longer than they probably should, based on what her brother had said.

"I'm not going out there," she muttered at last.

"You really should."

She shook her head, the tears she thought had dried up pricking behind her eyes. "I can't," Sophia whispered.

"What if I go with you?"

She huffed. "That wouldn't make it better."

He reached for her, prying her hand from her folded arms. When she finally looked at him, she noted the open concern in his gaze. "Playing devil's advocate... maybe you shouldn't make any rash decisions right now. Both of you are hurting."

"I can't believe you're defending him." Sophia attempted to pull her hand free, but her brother's grasp was too tight.

"I'm not defending him. All I'm saying is that life is complicated. It's messy. And until you both explore every possible avenue, you shouldn't give up. I've seen the way the two of you are together. I can see how much you love each other."

Her eyes slid to meet his.

Love.

There was that word again. Cameron had said he loved her. She'd wanted to believe it. She'd wanted to tell him she loved him, too. But something had held her back. It was like she was scared doing so would give him a piece of her heart she'd never get back.

"Just... talk to him. Okay?" Roman pleaded.

Sophia wanted to assure her brother that his words had helped, but she couldn't do that either. Nothing would fix this. And the fact that Cameron was here without first doing what she'd asked meant he hadn't heard her when they'd last spoken.

Roman rose from the bed at the same time as she did. When he moved to follow her down the stairs, she held up a hand. The last thing she wanted was for him to witness her severing the ties that connected her heart to Cameron's. It was for the best. And no number of second, third, or fiftieth chances was going to change that.

Sophia found Cameron sitting on the porch with his head in his hands. His hair was mussed so much it looked like he'd been tossed into a tornado. He snapped to his feet the second he heard the door shut.

Based on the bags under his eyes and the look of utter exhaustion on his face, she'd have to guess he hadn't slept at all last night.

Turned out they could still have something in common.

She grasped her hands at her back and stayed next to the door. She told herself it was because she wanted a quick escape if things went south, but the truth was more depressing. All she wanted to do was throw herself into his arms and beg him to agree to her terms so they could be together again.

Sophia's hands itched to run through his hair. Her arms

ached to wrap around his neck. She needed to kiss him, to assure not only him but also herself that everything would be okay.

But it wouldn't.

"Sophia," he rasped, taking a step closer.

She gave a sharp shake of her head and was relieved when he remained on the step where he stood. Her legs trembled but not as much as her voice. "We can't keep doing this to ourselves," she whispered.

He stepped closer again but then stopped himself. "I know you're upset. We both were—"

"This goes further than just being upset." Sophia fought the tears that threatened to spill again. "This is me finally accepting that the only way we're going to have a chance to come out of this as better people is if we work on ourselves. We can't do that when we're together."

"What are you saying?"

She shut her eyes to fight the mounting frustration. Forcing her voice to remain level, she said softly, "You know what I'm saying. I said it as plainly as I could yesterday." She opened her eyes, and a tear tumbled down her cheek. "We're toxic when we're together. We're jealous and maybe a little vindictive. Honestly, I'm surprised we lasted as long as we have."

"Those were just bad days," Cameron attempted with a broken voice. "I'll do better."

Sophia shook her head. That's just it. I want you to do better, but you can't when you're so focused on me." This time she moved to the edge of the porch so they were eye-to-eye, with him a step lower. "We need to break things off."

Cameron reached for her hand, and she let him. He laced his fingers between hers, staring at the way they were connected when he whispered, "I can't live without you. We're meant to be together. I know it in my heart."

"Maybe."

He lifted hopeful eyes to her, but he must have seen the resignation on her face because that hope was decimated in a matter of seconds.

"But not right now. We both have to work on ourselves first."

Muscles feathered in his jaw as he continued to stare up at her. For a moment, she expected him to lash out, to yell at her, scream, throw a tantrum like he had at the park. But he didn't. Cameron simply released her hand and took a step down to put space between them. "So this is what you want. To be free of me."

No. She didn't want that. Sophia wanted Cameron more than she'd wanted anyone else—even more than she'd wanted Brent. But she couldn't say that now. She couldn't give Cameron any reason to believe that there was another option beyond this breakup. In her heart, she knew they both needed this space. They needed to heal that broken part of their souls that made it so difficult to have a healthy relationship.

Then maybe, when enough time had passed, they would find each other.

She wrung her hands before her as she watched him shake his head and retreat even farther. The distance didn't just come physically. She could sense it emotionally, too. He was breaking. So was she.

And maybe this was like setting a broken bone. They needed to break one more time before they could be set right and heal properly.

"Goodbye, Cameron," she whispered. He probably didn't hear her.

Sophia's eyes followed him as he stalked toward his truck. He shut his door with far too much strength, and she winced. Then he peeled out of the driveway and his truck disappeared from view.

He still had a contract. They'd still have to work together.

Well, shoot. Mateo had been one hundred percent right.

24

———

Cameron

Miserable didn't come close to the way Cameron felt right now.

Five years ago, when Sophia had walked out of his life, he hadn't known what he'd be missing out on—not really. Now he was hyper aware of every little thing that he had lost.

She had to feel the same way.

He'd seen it in her eyes.

It had been a week since she'd told him he needed to get help. He didn't like it. He knew exactly what she meant. She wanted him to go to therapy.

Well, she was wrong.

Had he overreacted? Sure.

Multiple times? Yeah, and he wasn't proud of it.

But did that mean something was so inherently wrong with him that he needed to go to a shrink and talk about his feelings?

No!

Cameron's emotions ranged from heartache to fuming mad over the last couple of days. He wasn't going to see a therapist. What would they be able to say anyway? They'd probably tell him to confront his brother and tell Samuel exactly how he felt.

It wouldn't change anything. Samuel was the one who needed to change.

The horses seemed more skittish today than usual, and he knew the exact reason. They could sense his turmoil. That was one thing about animals that was both a blessing and a curse. Today, it was the latter and was making his job harder. He was distracted and grumpy.

It was probably best that he hadn't seen much of Sophia today. She'd been getting up earlier than him for the last day or two. And when he showed up to work, she made herself scarce. There was no chance of him talking to her when she managed to anticipate his every move.

He already had a plan. She needed space, but eventually he'd attempt to talk to her again. If he could get her alone, he'd be able to convince her that this whole situation was a big misunderstanding and she was overreacting.

Sophia had to understand that Cameron didn't have a choice after he'd found his brother at the scene. She knew what it meant to him—how it hurt him.

The following day, Sophia wasn't in the barn when he'd shown up to work. He didn't know if he'd missed her or if she had slept in. His answer came when Sophia ambled into the barn a few hours after he had.

She stopped short at the door, hesitated, then continued toward the saddles. "I'm taking Tilly for a ride. Seeing as she's not expecting, I didn't think that would be a problem."

He didn't know what got into him as he followed her to the saddles. "Sophia, we should talk."

"Have you started seeing a therapist?"

"No, but—"

"Then we don't have anything to discuss." She tightened the ponytail in her hair, then hefted the saddle and marched over to Tilly's stall.

"Yes, we do."

"I said everything I needed to say to you, Cameron. Unless you're ready to work on improving—"

He grasped her upper arm, stopping her in the middle of saddling Tilly. She stopped and stared down at where he was touching her. She frowned.

"Please... Sophia. Talk to me."

"Let. Go." Her tone had him reeling. This was not the woman he'd fallen in love with. She was broken. There was pain in her voice. Desperation, perhaps? And anger.

Cameron fought the instinct to flinch at the tone. He didn't release her. "I miss you," he whispered.

That caught her off guard. She stared at him for a moment, her eyes flickering with so many emotions that he couldn't keep any of them straight. He'd hoped that she'd say she missed him too. Or that she'd be willing to hear him out. Instead, she shook her head and pulled away from him.

She led Tilly from the barn, and he continued to follow her, but he was stopped in his tracks when Mateo and Roman blocked his path. Mateo looked disappointed and maybe a little irritated. Roman almost looked sad.

"Let her go, Cameron," Roman said.

"You know I can't do that."

Mateo folded his arms. "I've kept out of this up until this

point, but I can't let you keep doing this. She told you what she wanted. You have to respect her wishes."

Cameron could feel the desperation growing within him. Frustration, too. These guys didn't know what they were talking about. They only had Sophia's side of the story. How could they understand if they didn't hear him out?

He frowned at one man, then the next. "I just need to talk to her. I think if I can explain—"

"What is there to explain?" Mateo said quietly. "You attacked your brother."

"He *kissed* her," Cameron snapped. "He kissed her, and he was trying to—"

The pity in Roman's eyes only fueled Cameron's fury. "That doesn't give you an excuse to do what you did. He's your flesh and blood. And from what I understand, he didn't even know the two of you were together."

"And that's my fault?"

"No one said that it's your fault. But you're responsible for your own choices." Why did Mateo have to be the voice of reason right now? What he was saying made a great deal of sense, and Cameron hated it.

Yes, he was responsible for his own choices. Yes, he needed to rein himself in. But his brother should have known better.

"You need to leave her alone, Cameron. I know it's going to be hard, but you can't just keep chasing after her." Roman placed a hand on Cameron's shoulder, and it took everything in his power not to shrug him off or push him away.

Cameron opened his mouth to argue, but Roman continued.

"You want to get her back, right?"

"You know I do," Cameron shot back, his eyes drifting to where Sophia had disappeared. "I'll do anything—"

"Including seeing a therapist?"

Cameron's mouth clamped shut. Anything but that. What was a therapist supposed to help him do? Cameron didn't need to sit down on some uncomfortable chair and talk out his feelings. He needed his brother to admit he was just trying to make his life miserable. Once he confessed, no one would look at Cameron like he was the bad guy.

"I know you don't like that idea, but Sophia is right." Mateo's words dragged Cameron back to the present conversation. "And honestly? I think it would be a good idea for you while you work here."

"Seeing a therapist isn't in my contract," Cameron ground out. "I'm not required to do any such thing." He was fully aware that he was pushing his luck with his boss. He just couldn't dredge up the ability to care.

The look on Mateo's face made it clear that Cameron was right, but Mateo wasn't happy about it. He probably would require therapy if they were to extend the contract.

Cameron folded his arms, looking from one man to the other. "If that's everything..."

Roman glanced at his brother, then back to Cameron. "Just leave her alone. She's already said that she's going to do the same. You guys need space."

"I don't need space," Cameron argued. "All I need is her. I'm not going to hurt anyone else. I'm not going to lose my temper."

"Of course not," Mateo said bitterly. "Because if you do, then I'll have to void our contract. I won't allow anyone on my payroll who is a danger to themselves or others. I don't care about your excuses." He didn't have to say his threat outright. Mateo's message was loud and clear.

There would be no more flexibility when it came to Cameron's jealous outbursts.

Clearly, Cameron had been lucky up to this point regarding what Mateo was willing to put up with. He got the feeling that if Mateo was completely informed of every altercation, that would change.

Cameron dragged a hand down his face. "It won't happen again," he attempted to reassure the man who he also considered a friend. "I just..." He sighed. "Please. Let me talk to her. One more time."

Mateo shook his head, as did his brother. They weren't going to budge an inch when it came to their sister, and Cameron couldn't blame them. If the roles were reversed, he'd do the same. That didn't mean it wasn't frustrating as all get-out.

Cameron gritted his jaw tight. Mateo and Roman wouldn't let him see Sophia if they were around when he got to her, but they couldn't always play gatekeeper. Eventually, she'd have to talk to him. Eventually, she'd have to accept that they were endgame, no matter how much she wanted to fight it.

He marched back to his station and continued with his work. Knowing Sophia, she wouldn't be coming around any time soon. By the time she got back, Cameron might not even be here. She'd managed to elude him again.

Busying himself with the horses, he took his time grooming them and checking them over for any injuries or problematic issues. Mateo's family took good care of the animals on their property. They knew how important it was to maintain a certain standard of cleanliness and health for the breeding process. It wasn't the only reason he'd agreed to work with Mateo, but it was certainly a big one.

His thoughts drifted to Sophia more often than not, and he found himself grimacing at some of the nonsense he'd allowed himself to participate in. While there were some instances he regretted, there were others that he simply couldn't bring himself to feel guilt over. Sophia was the love of his life, and he wanted everyone to know it.

Was it so bad that he was protective of her? Wasn't that what women wanted? At least she didn't have any doubt as to whether he was interested in her or not—unlike him. With how *friendly* Sophia was with other men, he found himself wondering if she was content with what they had together.

That thought soured his stomach. He'd told her he trusted her. But maybe that was part of the problem. He *didn't* trust her as much as he should, and he could definitely work on that part of the problem.

Just as expected, he wrapped things up before Sophia returned from her ride. He didn't know what she did all day out with the horse, but he was glad to see her home safe. He'd been tempted to jog out to the barn when she disappeared inside, but just as soon as he took a step in that direction, Roman materialized out of nowhere.

Cameron groaned. He'd thought the five years of not knowing who she was had been bad. But having her, only to let her slip through his fingers, was exponentially worse. He settled back on the steps to the wranglers' cabin, his forearms resting atop his knees. He simply needed a better plan to get to her.

Maybe he'd be able to catch her when she went out with

her friends. She'd done that a lot before they'd started dating. Eventually, she'd do it again.

25

———

Sophia

"I can't believe I let you drag me out here," Sophia said to Camilla. Her sister had insisted that she just wanted to get something to eat at the restaurant in the country club. She'd put Sophia on a huge guilt trip to do it, too.

"You and I both know that you needed to get out of the house," Camilla said over the music coming through the speakers in the ballroom.

"I get out of the house," Sophia scoffed.

"I don't mean those horse rides you've been taking," her sister said pointedly. "You've been miserable."

"Gee. Thanks," Sophia deadpanned.

Camilla nudged her and gestured to the large gathering that had come out to the club for dancing. An upbeat country song played and most everyone had found a partner to swing them around the dance floor. Her sister had a wide smile on her face. "I told Emma to meet us here, too. You don't have to be alone. And you don't have to hang out with any guys." Camilla wrinkled her nose. "It can be a girls' night."

It had been a couple weeks since Sophia had ended things with Cameron, and based on what she could tell, he wasn't making any efforts to improve himself. He hovered at the ranch, his eyes always finding her wherever she was. He'd had a few talks with her brothers—none of which her brothers felt she needed to bother herself with.

Sophia, on the other hand, had done what she'd insisted Cameron do. She'd found a therapist who could help her through the scars of her past—those that made it hard for her to give herself completely to a relationship.

There were days she felt like she was returning to normal. Then something would happen, and she'd feel the pain of losing Cameron all over again. She hated the good days just as much as she hated the bad ones—mostly because she knew they wouldn't last.

Her heart still ached for Cameron. She wanted nothing more than to run back into his arms and give him the second chance he wanted. Maybe this time would be different.

But then she reminded herself that if Cameron wasn't willing to do the work, nothing would change. It was hard— seeing a therapist—harder than Sophia had anticipated. But it was helping.

Someone pulled on her arm, and she glanced over at her sister. "Come on. Let's get out there. You need to laugh and smile again."

Sophia rolled her eyes. "I'm fine, Camilla. I don't need to dance to feel better."

Her sister placed her hands on her hips. "If it was Emma who was dealing with a breakup, what would you say?"

"I'd ask her what she needed and make it happen."

"Don't lie. I can always tell when you're lying. You'd tell Emma that she needed to get back out there, and if she didn't listen to you, you'd make her do it."

Camilla wasn't wrong, but Sophia wasn't about to tell her that. It would ruin any chance of going home early.

Placing a hand to her stomach, Sophia pretended that it was unsettled. "I ate too much. I don't think I can—"

With a groan, Camilla yanked Sophia's arm and tugged her toward the dance floor without another word. Sophia had no choice. Her first movements were stilted and heavy. She didn't feel like dancing. She just wanted to crawl under the covers and pretend that the last several months hadn't happened. She'd been just fine before Cameron had entered her life. But as much as she hated to admit it, she couldn't deny that even though he'd made things difficult at times, she still loved him.

She ached for him. For that smile. For his warm hugs. For every kiss and knowing look that passed between them.

The dance was torture. Sophia barely made it through without wanting to dart for the door and call herself an Uber. But then she felt it.

She felt *him.*

Despite the room being crowded, she could sense that Cameron was there. She didn't know how he figured out she had come tonight—then again, she wouldn't be surprised if he'd been watching her. He seemed to constantly be doing that.

Her gaze flitted through the room, darting from corner to corner, group to group, until they landed on him.

His eyes locked with hers from where he leaned against the wall with his arms folded. His face was a mask of utter unreadability, but those eyes said so much more. How was it possible that in his eyes, she could see the desire, the pain, and the hope he had swirling all at once? No other eyes had been nearly as expressive as his.

She took a step in his direction, then halted, shook her head, and spun away from him. She moved off to join the group Emma and Camilla were in. They were talking animatedly about a tour Emma's manager wanted her to take next year.

"You have to go."

Emma laughed. "And what would I do with my kid? I can guarantee that Caleb won't let me go alone. There is literally no way."

Camilla shrugged. "I'm sure we could figure out something. You married into one of the biggest families there is here. And my family wouldn't be totally against babysitting."

Their eyes found Sophia, and Camilla frowned.

"What's wrong? You look like you've seen a ghost."

Sophia nearly told them that she felt like she had. She was so tempted to point out the reason for her unease but thought better of it. She knew they wouldn't do anything to make matters worse. They were her cheerleaders. If Sophia had told them she wanted to give it another try with Cameron, they'd probably tell her to go for it while at the same time telling her to be careful.

That's not what she needed right now.

She needed someone to help her keep a clear head. The second Cameron spoke to her, she knew she was a goner. She wasn't strong enough for this.

Sophia shook her head and swallowed hard.

"Do you need to go home? Are you sick?" Emma questioned.

Again, Sophia shook her head. "No, but I think I need to get some air. I'll be right back."

She realized her mistake the second she reached the railing of the balcony off the dance floor.

"Sophia," Cameron's low, husky voice reached her, sending all kinds of chills and goosebumps rippling on her body.

Squeezing her eyes shut as tight as she could, she forced herself not to react to him. She couldn't let her guard down. She wouldn't.

"Sophia," he pleaded. "Can we talk?"

She pressed her lips together tight, her teeth biting into them as she considered all her options. She could dart away from him, head back inside and demand that Emma or Camilla take her home. She could sit there and ignore him. She could face this head-on and do her best to remain strong.

She'd missed him so much. It wasn't fair that he was here, asking her to speak to him.

His fingers grazed her upper arm, and she jerked backward.

The pain in his eyes was knee-buckling.

"What do you want, Cameron?" She'd tried sounding sharp and angry, but the question came out as more of a whimper.

"I want another chance—"

Sophia shook her head. "I can't do that. *We* can't do that."

"Why not?" he demanded. "I've given you space. I'm working on myself—"

"Are you seeing someone? A therapist?"

The way his expression hardened was all the answer she needed.

"Cameron, we can't."

His brows pulled together, but rather than anger, she saw concern. He reached toward her and miraculously, she didn't retreat. The calloused pad of his thumb wiped at the apple of her cheek, brushing a tear from her skin. Her breath shuddered as his eyes returned to meet hers. "You're upset."

The pain and loss of it all had consumed her for so long that all she had left was anger. She swatted his hand from her face. "Of course I'm upset. I'm heartbroken. Because I want nothing more than to be with you. I love you, Cameron—"

"Then give us a chance."

"Don't you understand? The cycle will only continue. Sure, you could make little improvements now on your own, but eventually..." She heaved a sad sigh and forced herself to meet his eyes with a steady stare. "Eventually you'll revert back to the person that you're most comfortable with. Unless you're willing to make a change, develop better habits, nothing is going to stick."

She wasn't innocent in all of this either, but at least she'd seen what she needed to do to fix it. Making time for therapy wasn't easy. It was tedious, and sometimes it didn't feel like she was making any progress on her healing. But she planned to stick with it. She still had insecurities that flared up.

His frown turned into something of a scowl. Cameron might not be voicing it, but he clearly didn't believe he needed help.

There was nothing she could do to change his mind. It

hurt knowing that if she chose to wait for him, she might be left hanging indefinitely.

Before he could get past her weakening defenses with his touches, his smile, or those pleading eyes, she brushed past him.

Emma and Camilla weren't where they'd been seated before. And Sophia could feel Cameron's presence behind her as she headed into the crowd. A slow song started, and her heart pounded angrily in her chest. She was desperate. She couldn't be stuck dancing with him. One touch was all it would take to melt her hardened heart like butter.

She latched onto the first cowboy she found. "Want to dance?"

His surprise was short-lived.

As was her relief when he agreed.

Ugh! She'd resorted to being with another guy in front of Cameron. Again.

Only this time, it wasn't to feed off his jealousy. This was out of self-preservation.

The stranger slipped his hands around her waist and smiled at her. He was objectively attractive and that flirtatious smile only added to it. He had brilliant blue eyes that normally would have had her pulse fluttering.

But all she could think about were the dark eyes that were drilling into the side of her face. Cameron wasn't in the middle of the dance floor. He leaned against the wall at the side of the room. When she glanced at him, she noted his stiff stance and his arms folded tight at his chest.

He continued to stare at her, his jaw flexing. A girl approached and Sophia looked away. Cameron didn't belong to her anymore. He could dance with another girl even if the thought of it made her sick to her stomach.

She was such a hypocrite.

When she glanced in his direction once more, she found he hadn't left with the girl. She was gone, but he remained. What was he trying to express? That he would rather be alone and miserable, watching her in someone else's arms, than try something new with someone else?

No. She couldn't believe that.

The Cameron she knew was obsessive, and he simply hadn't found a new plaything to focus his obsession on.

He didn't bother coming up to her when the dance ended. In fact, he kept his distance. He didn't even dance with anyone else.

The worst part was that every time she took on another dance partner, she saw the emotions warring in Cameron's eyes—even from where she stood on the dance floor. There was pain—heartache—in those eyes of his. Perhaps she saw a little bit of fury, as well.

And it wasn't until she made it home and was lying in her bed staring at the ceiling that one thing became clear in her head.

She'd gone over the night again and again. One thing stood out.

Cameron had been restrained.

He hadn't cut in to any of her dances with other men. He hadn't lost his temper. He hadn't put her down for letting another guy hold her during a slow song.

Sophia sat up in bed and leaned against the headboard. His behavior was so different from what she was familiar with. While he hadn't gone out and found a therapist, he was still working to better himself. She knew from experience how hard it must have been for him to simply stand back and watch as she attempted to move on.

Guilt coursed through her veins. She didn't owe him anything. She shouldn't be experiencing these feelings. Cameron had dug his hole. She'd given him the tools to get himself out, and he was still refusing.

And yet, there was a trickle of hope in the despair that she felt over losing what she'd had.

She groaned, placing her head in her hands. She couldn't falter. She couldn't show weakness. This was for the best. Cameron needed to want to make the change in order for it to stick.

She just hoped that when he found that better part of himself, he wouldn't hold this against her.

26

———

Cameron

Cameron hadn't planned on spending any additional time with Sophia's brothers. After the night at the country club, he decided that he wasn't going to push Sophia anymore. He'd lost. That much was clear.

He'd resigned himself to finishing out his contract with Mateo and then he'd get out of Copper Creek and disappear. She wouldn't have to see him anymore. She wouldn't have to look at him like the monster he was.

And yet, here he sat in the coffee shop across from Roman.

He must be a glutton for punishment because this was the last place in the world Cameron wanted to be. He stared hard at his coffee cup. He'd been caught off guard enough to accept Roman's offer when they bumped into each other in town.

What had he been thinking? Roman probably hated

him. Why was he insisting that they have a chat? They could have talked a hundred times over since the last time he'd refused to grant access to his sister.

Why now?

What had changed in the last two weeks?

"Are you going to talk or just stare daggers at your coffee?" Roman quipped.

Cameron lifted his sour gaze to the man seated in front of him. "I'm not the one who issued the invitation to coffee."

"No, but I know you want something."

Eyes narrowing, Cameron scoffed. "You can't be serious. What is this? Some sort of carrot you're dangling in front of me? I might still want Sophia more than breath itself, but that doesn't mean I get to have her. She made her choice." He reached for his cup and moved to stand, but Roman's words cut through him like a sharpened blade.

"She's not happy."

Cameron's eyes flitted back to Roman's face, half-expecting to see fury there. Glee perhaps? Anything but the concern and pain that was currently shining in his eyes. He shifted back into a more comfortable position and waited expectantly for Roman to continue.

The man sighed and rubbed at the back of his neck. "She's miserable, honestly. She misses you."

Straightening slightly, Cameron allowed himself the smallest glimmer of hope. "Does she want me back—"

"No."

His expression faltered, and Cameron scowled at the man. "Then what in heaven's name are we here to talk about?"

Roman waved a finger in Cameron's direction. "She doesn't want this version."

Cameron scoffed.

"She was right, you know. There are a few things you need to work on before you try to win her back. She's made that perfectly clear. You can't keep behaving like you did when you knocked your brother to the ground."

It was hard to meet Roman's eyes. Hot, mortifying disgust ripped through his body as he recalled the way his brother had looked at him from the ground. That had been rock bottom, and Cameron had known it. Since then, he'd focused all his energies on remaining calm—no easy feat when all he saw was the woman he loved in the arms of others.

"There's nothing I can do about that, Roman," he said quietly.

The man before him snorted, then choked on the coffee he'd been drinking. He pounded his chest and shook his head. "If you truly believe that, you're an idiot. She practically gave you step-by-step instructions."

"What? That therapy suggestion?" Cameron snapped.

"It wasn't a suggestion," Roman said. "It was a good idea. You need it."

Cameron didn't bother responding to that statement. He wasn't a psychopath. Did he get jealous? Yeah. Had he overreacted with his brother? Perhaps. But he'd gone over that day in his head, and for the most part he felt he was in the right. His brother had all but stolen the affection of his first girlfriend. And he'd been at it again. It wasn't unheard of for Cameron to do something to protect what belonged to him.

"Stop that," Roman grumbled.

"Stop what?" Cameron hissed. His eyes bore into Roman's with a challenge.

"Stop making excuses for yourself. I can tell that's what

you're doing, and no matter how you try to spin it, you're wrong. Sophia deserves better."

Cameron shot to his feet, his palms rattling the table as he leaned over and glowered at Roman. "Don't you think I know that? She deserves the best. And me? I don't even begin to get close to it. I was lucky she gave me a chance at all." He was breathing heavily, and several people in the coffee shop were looking at them now. His eyes darted around the room before he slowly lowered himself back into his seat. Then he leaned forward. "And if you think therapy will change that, *you're* the idiot, not me."

Roman didn't seem fazed in the slightest. "Why are you so scared about talking to someone?"

Cameron settled back in his seat. He wanted to say he wasn't, that being scared of a therapist was absurd. But that wouldn't be true.

He was scared to open himself up to something like that, only because he didn't think it would do any good and he'd end up discovering that he was broken beyond repair. He shifted his focus to the coffee cup and turned it in his fingertips. "Did Sophia tell you about how we met?"

If Roman seemed surprised over the change in topic, he didn't show it. "Something about a convention a couple years ago."

Cameron nodded. "I knew from the moment I saw her that she was special. I knew I wanted to sweep her off her feet and live happily ever after with her." He could feel the warmth crawling up the back of his neck at such a confession. "I was ready to follow her to the ends of the earth if it meant she would be mine." He leveled a firm stare at Roman. "Less than a week, Roman. That was all it took for her to steal my heart. And then she was gone."

Roman frowned. "Sorry, man."

Shrugging, Cameron shifted his thoughts back to Roman's original question. "It hurt, but it had been irrational to have such feelings anyway. That's what I told myself. Then I found her again, and I had been living in fear that I'd lose her again. It was like I had been barely breathing during those five years while I looked for her. Then when I saw her at your place, oxygen was breathed into my lungs and my chest didn't hurt anymore." He clutched at his chest with a fist, his eyes closing with the ache that rested beneath the surface. "My heart has been yanked around from the moment I met her. It's not her fault. And I know I have my own issues. But..."

Roman remained quiet throughout the story. He didn't push even as the silence between them stretched.

"But what if I do what she says and it's still not enough?" His voice cracked. "What if I do everything she wants and she still can't love me."

"That won't happen," Roman said, drawing Cameron's focus. "Because she's *still* in love with you."

Cameron shook his head in clear argument. He didn't have to tell Roman that Sophia had reverted to her old ways. She'd started going out again, flirting and dancing with any man who gave her attention. It made Cameron sick to his stomach. He couldn't handle the attention of other women. So he hadn't gone back to the country club even though he knew that was where Sophia would be throughout the week.

"Yes, she is. She's trying to cope. She's trying to give you space. But..." Roman sighed. "I shouldn't be telling you this."

Cameron waited, holding his breath as if the next thing Roman would say would be enough to stop the world from spinning.

"I've heard her crying. A few times." Roman flushed and stared over to the door as it opened, and a pretty blonde entered.

Crying? That didn't mean she was crying over him.

"I've never seen her this torn up over a guy. Not even Brent."

Cameron bristled. He hated that name more than he hated his brother for what he'd done to him.

"All I'm saying is that you need to reconsider this whole therapy thing."

Grimacing, Cameron halfway snatched his coffee from the table and took a drink.

"Okay, let me ask you this. If seeing a therapist meant winning Sophia back would be a sure thing, would you do it?"

"Of course," Cameron snapped. "But that's just it. There are no guarantees."

"You're right. There aren't any guarantees. But there is the chance that she'll take you back." Roman gave him a pointed look. "Cameron, that isn't the reason you should go."

He lowered his gaze, hating the turn this conversation had taken.

"You'd do anything for her, right?" Roman asked.

"Yeah," he ground out.

Roman sighed. "Why can't you do the same for yourself?"

Slowly, Cameron lifted his gaze to Roman.

"She wants you to get better—to get over whatever it is that's holding you back. If you're willing to do anything for her. Then make that happen." He lifted placating palms. "That's all I wanted to say." Roman glanced once more to the blonde who'd entered a little while ago. They exchanged smiles, and she looked as though she wanted to stop by their table to talk to him.

Was she a potential girlfriend? Or just an acquaintance?

It didn't matter. She slipped past them with nothing more than a nod in Roman's direction. Roman's eyes followed her out the door before returning to Cameron.

"Anyway, if you decide you need a recommendation, I'm sure I could help you find someone. And if you decide you hate my advice?" He shrugged. "Then I guess we know where the cards have fallen." He got to his feet and retrieved the hat he'd placed on the chair at his side. "Just think about it, okay? I don't like seeing my sister hurt so much."

Cameron grunted. He didn't stand or watch Roman leave. He just stared at his still mostly full coffee cup.

He'd watched her with all those guys last weekend. And each time he'd had to shove his hands deep into his pockets to stop himself from intervening. It had taken all his energy to not pull her into his arms when he'd gotten her alone. He'd felt like a fool afterward—the way he'd begged her to take him back.

At least he hadn't taken a swing at anyone. And he hadn't dragged her out of there caveman-style. That was an improvement, right?

Maybe Roman was right.

Cameron had tried every other avenue. Perhaps this therapy thing was the route he'd have to take.

27

———

Sophia

Sophia headed out of the grocery store with one bag in hand and nearly collided with Sam. She gasped and stumbled back a step. He was quick, grasping her wrist before she knocked into someone else.

A wry smile played on his lips. The bruising on his face from his brother was still present, but it was fading into that brownish-green color.

She grimaced, reaching up as if she were going to touch the injuries, but then thought better of herself.

Samuel released her hand and shoved both of his into his pockets. "I was hoping I'd bump into you today," he said.

She glanced around warily. Cameron must have done a number on her if she was concerned he'd be coming out of the woodwork to do more damage. When she didn't immediately sense any impending danger, she brought her eyes back to Sam. "You could have called."

He lifted a shoulder. "And would you have answered?"

Biting back a chagrined smile, she shook her head. "Probably not."

"And seeing as he's working for your brother... I thought it best not to just show up at your property."

Heat filled her face. Sam didn't have to say Cameron's name for her to know who he was talking about. Cameron was the topic of most of her conversations lately despite how much she wanted to avoid them.

She cleared her throat and shifted her weight from one foot to the other. "I'm really sorry... about what happened. I should have told you I was seeing him."

"I didn't exactly give you a chance to get a word in about it."

"But I could have said I was dating. I don't know what I was thinking, not telling you."

Sam chuckled. If he was upset with her, he wasn't showing it. "It's my fault, too."

She scoffed. "How is getting beaten up your fault? Your brother should have known better. He should have—"

He placed a warm, firm hand on her forearm. "I don't know if he told you anything about our past, but I wasn't exactly the best big brother to him."

Sophia attempted to hide that she knew exactly what he was talking about. The truth was, she only knew one side of the story, and while she sympathized with Cameron, those sympathies were waning when she saw the way Cameron went after his brother.

Sam chuckled again, but this time it sounded strained—embarrassed, even. "Cam fell hard and fast for this girl in high school. I swear, my brother thought the moon rose and fell on Kristy. I could tell that she wasn't completely into him. It was obvious that she would have willingly gone off to the next guy if the opportunity presented itself. I told Cameron as much, but he got upset."

Sophia's brows rose. This wasn't part of the story she knew.

Blowing out a breath, Samuel continued. "So, I decided to save him the heartache and intervene. I flirted with her one time. One time, Sophia. And that was all it took for her to kiss me. I don't know if it was the fact that I was older. Or that I was her boyfriend's brother. Whatever the reason, she threw herself at me and Cameron found out. Rumors got out of control, and Cameron believed them all. They said I was the aggressor in that relationship." Sam's eyes were almost pleading as he lowered his voice. "He was heartbroken, and I knew if I corrected the rumors and told him the truth, it would destroy him. I didn't think he'd overcome the betrayal, and I didn't want him to become jaded in the relationship department."

She stared at him blankly. So much pain had been locked between them and all because Sam had wanted to protect Cameron from a girl who didn't deserve him.

He shrugged again. "I probably should have just told him. Clearly, trying to shelter him was just as bad as the other outcome could have been. Eventually, he forgave me—on the surface, at least. But the damage had been done."

Her head was reeling. "Why can't you tell him now?"

"I doubt he'd listen. Especially after what happened between the two of us." He gave her a sad smile. "I'm so sorry, Sophia."

"You don't have to apologize," she insisted. "What happened between Cameron and me is... for the best." At least she hoped so. She was starting to question herself more and more the longer they were apart. Samuel didn't know her as well as some, and it was likely even he could hear that she didn't believe what she was saying. "For the record, I think you should come clean to Cameron. He has spent this whole time believing you were the bad guy."

"But I was."

She gave him a pointed look—one she hoped conveyed just how much she didn't believe that. Had he gone about it the wrong way? Sure. But he hadn't been trying to hurt his brother. He'd been trying to help.

Samuel only shrugged. "I don't know that talking to him would do much good. And after what happened? I'm already worried about seeing him today."

Her brows shot upward. "You're seeing him today?"

The nervous look he gave her made her stomach twist in knots. It wasn't like she hadn't seen Cameron recently. She didn't know why his statement put her on edge. Cameron had caught Sam off guard when he'd started throwing punches. This time, he wouldn't be so lucky. "Do you know why?"

It was none of her business, of course. Sam didn't have to tell her anything. She held her breath as she waited for him to respond, then exhaled when he did.

He rubbed the back of his neck—a nervous habit he'd had when they'd spent time together a couple years ago. "Honestly, I don't know. I had no plans for coming back to Copper Creek any time soon—especially since Cameron is staying here for the next little while." He blew out a breath and chuckled. "Cameron asked me to come, and I guess my morbid curiosity got the better of me. Maybe I'm a glutton for punishment or something."

That brought a smile to Sophia's face even though it

probably shouldn't have. She could relate to that. After everything that Cameron did that rubbed her the wrong way, Sophia was still drawn to him.

Sam offered her another smile. "Anyway, I'm gonna head out. Don't want to be late to that coffee, right?"

She nodded. Samuel looked like he was about to lean in for a hug, but then he held himself back. It wasn't hard to figure out what he was thinking in that moment. The last time they'd touched, he'd been knocked to the ground. It was fine. A hug now would have been more than awkward. "See you around, Sam."

"Yeah, see ya around."

Sophia watched him as he moved past her and headed across the street to the coffee shop. Her curiosity got the better of her, and as much as she knew she shouldn't, she followed after him.

She slipped into the building, first taking stock to find that Cameron wasn't present. Sam was already in a booth, staring at his phone. Without thinking about it too long, Sophia moved in that direction. She ducked down into the seat of a booth behind him. Based on the height of the booth chairs, no one would know she was there unless they moved to the bathroom at the back of the shop.

Thankfully, Sam was distracted enough that he hadn't even seen Sophia move past him.

Her heart beat wildly in her chest as she waited for Cameron to arrive. When she heard the sound of his voice, she went stock-still. Though he spoke quietly, she could hear everything he said.

"Thanks for meeting with me."

"What can I say? I was curious."

A chuckle. Then strained silence.

"So, what is it? You want to tell me I'm the cause of all your problems? Blame me for the mess you found yourself in?" Samuel shifted in his seat, and the leather beneath him creaked with the movement.

Sophia waited with bated breath. She closed her eyes, expecting Cameron to do just that. But then he shocked her.

"I'm sorry."

She squirmed in her seat, turning her head so she could hear him better.

Cameron sighed. "I was wrong. I let my temper get the better of me. I overreacted and I... Let's just say there's room for improvement."

Sam let out a low whistle. "I can't say I expected *that*."

"Yeah, well... I'm trying to be... better."

"For her?"

There was more silence, and then Cameron sighed. Sophia could imagine him running a hand through his mussed hair or dragging it down his face. Then Cameron said, "No. Not for her. I mean, sure—if she'd take me back, I want to be someone she deserves. But right now? I'm just trying to fix my mistakes. For me."

Sophia's heart practically trembled in her chest. She closed her eyes and didn't realize the tears were falling until one dropped from her chin and landed on her hand. There was no way he knew she was seated here, but that could change at any given moment.

She didn't want to be caught. Suddenly, listening to their conversation felt like an invasion of privacy. So, she scrunched down as low onto the bench as she could and prayed that he wouldn't need to use the restroom before she could slip out unnoticed.

Thankfully, in less than ten minutes, it happened. The

brothers left on better terms than they'd arrived. Samuel didn't tell Cameron what he'd confessed to Sophia, and he might never do so. But Sophia couldn't think about that right now.

Her thoughts were consumed with the fact that Cameron had taken a step in the right direction without being told to do so.

~

"You've been quiet."

Sophia glanced up at Emma. "Have I?"

She laughed. "We've literally gone into three stores, and you haven't said a single thing. What's going on? Is Cameron still hassling you?"

"The contrary, actually." Sophia had paid more attention to him lately. She'd begun to notice little changes he'd been making in his behavior. They'd bump into each other at the country club when she'd been around town, and he was simply... different. He gave her space even when other guys were obviously hitting on her. He didn't even seem angry anymore.

It wasn't that he didn't care. She could still see the look of desire in his eyes. That smoldering look said it all. His feelings for her hadn't changed. But Cameron had.

Sophia swallowed and offered her friend a smile. "Sorry."

Emma opened her mouth to say something as they continued on their way down the street but immediately snapped it shut as her eyes landed on something over Sophia's shoulder. Sophia glanced in that direction and gasped.

Cameron smiled at her. It had been nearly a month since his apology to his brother, and he was looking good.

More than good, he looked like he was glowing—as much as a guy could.

Wow! Her brain wasn't willing to work for her when this mouth-watering specimen looked at her like that.

"Sophia," Cameron said, his voice slipping past her defenses and making her legs turn into mush.

"Hey," she rasped, then cleared her throat. "How are you doing?"

"I'm gonna get us some muffins at the bakery. I'll be right back," Emma said.

Before Sophia could demand that her friend stay by her side, Emma had disappeared. Sophia looked after her like she was doomed before lifting her gaze to Cameron.

That smile made her want to do things—say things—she had no business participating in. She chewed on the inside of her cheek to prevent herself from putting her foot in her mouth, but apparently her head didn't get the memo. "You look good," she blurted. It was silly. She'd seen him around at the ranch even though she'd managed to avoid him more often than not.

"Thanks. You don't look half bad yourself."

She flushed with embarrassment. This had to be the most awkward conversation ever. There was so much she could say to him right now. The temptation to tell him she wanted to start over nearly burst from her when he completely shattered her reality.

He shifted, running a hand through his hair. "I started seeing someone."

Her stomach dropped. "You have?" Her voice was just

above a whisper, and she hated how the jealousy in her chest jarred her reality.

"Yeah, he's pretty great. He works with some of the veterans over at the country club. Holds a group meeting for people with anger issues, too."

Her heartache immediately shifted to understanding, and she bit back a surprised laugh. "You're seeing a therapist?"

Cameron nodded, embarrassment written all over his face. "It's been good, though. You were right."

"I'm so happy for you!" Sophia stepped forward. "That's amazing." Cameron was really doing it. It took every ounce of her self-control not to tell him what had been on her mind. She couldn't exactly ask him out when he'd just admitted to seeing a therapist. How would that go over?

Not well.

It'd look like Sophia only wanted him back because he was doing what she'd recommended. He might not even be interested in taking her back anymore. He'd changed.

She blinked away the tears that stung behind her eyes. Sophia would have to let him go. It was the right thing to do. Swallowing back the disappointment, she forced a smile. "I'm so proud of you."

He hovered there. For a moment she thought he might say something more, but he didn't.

"Sophia! Ready?"

They both looked over to where Emma was holding up a brown paper sack from the bakery.

"I should probably..." Sophia murmured.

Cameron nodded. "I'll see you around. At work."

"Right," Sophia agreed. "At work." She smiled and then pushed past him. Her skin brushed against his and a chill ripped through her body. No looking back. She wouldn't be able to bear it without running into his arms. She wouldn't become the reason he got derailed from the improvements he'd started to make.

He was happy. Who was she to upend that?

28

Cameron

"How have your exercises been going?"

Cameron glanced up from his hands. His therapist sat with his ankle across his knee. He was the epitome of attentiveness, without making Cameron feel like he was digging for something to judge him on. It had been easy for Cameron to trust the guy. But they'd been going at this for a couple weeks and he still didn't feel he was at the point where he could try again with Sophia. "Good, I guess."

"You think things could improve?"

He held back a sigh. His whole body itched to move on from the breathing techniques and the positive self-affirmations. Deep down, he knew he'd be just as scared to lose Sophia if she were to give him another chance, and he didn't know if he'd survive losing her again after that. "I feel like I've hit a wall with all of it."

"You don't think you've improved?"

"I know I have." Cameron settled in his seat and rested his head against the back of the couch. "That's not the problem."

"Then what's the problem?"

With a ragged brush of his hand through his hair, Cameron shut his eyes and willed his heart to slow. "I keep seeing her around town, at work…" Even in his dreams. "And it's getting harder and harder not to beg her to take me back. I'm not good enough for her. I know the second she does, I'll revert to the person I was when we were together."

"And why do you think that is?" Tyson prodded.

Cameron blew out a heavy breath. "Because I know it's only a matter of time before I'll lose her to someone better."

Tanner was quiet for a moment. There wasn't a change in his easy expression—no indication of what he was thinking at the moment. He might as well be wearing a mask with the unreadability of his brown eyes and dark brows. Tanner gave himself a short nod before commenting. "We all have insecurities, guilt, shame, anxieties. They're the parts of us that hold us back—for good or for bad. For instance, we need a moral compass. Without shame and guilt, we'd have no reason to care for others and the way they feel. But our insecurities are something of our own making. They're the shackles that hold us back based on our bad experiences. Unfortunately, most of those experiences were brought on by no fault of our own, and yet there is a part of us that clings to them like a lifeline. It's a strange sort of reflex if you think about it."

Cameron listened with half an ear. His experiences were rooted in the way his brother had treated him. Samuel had never truly made amends for what he'd done back then. They'd simply pretended like it had never happened. But

Tanner was right. Cameron still clung to the chains of that experience in a way. He let the pain from that moment in time strangle him when he was with Sophia. "How do I break the habit?"

"Well, what do you think are the root causes of those insecurities?"

"We've been through that—"

"Yes, you've mentioned your brother. Tell me why, after so many years, you still cling to it. Why haven't you forgiven him?"

"I have..." Cameron insisted, but his voice betrayed him. "Mostly."

"What would it take to break free of the shackles that bind that part of you—the side of you that becomes desperate—to your brother?"

He really wished his brother would acknowledge what had happened and apologize—explain, maybe. Samuel had never been cruel in their younger years.

"You don't have to answer out loud. It appears you have some idea as to what might help, and I suggest you explore that. Until then, continue with the exercises we've been working on. Remaining calm. Finding a place of peace when your anxiety becomes too much."

Cameron nodded. Maybe it was time to finally bury the hatchet with his brother.

"Tell me about Sophia."

Glancing up at Tanner, Cameron hesitated. They'd agreed that he needed to maintain his distance for Sophia's sake. But he'd been making excuses to see her or bump into her lately. Tanner wouldn't approve. He cleared his throat. "I'm still in love with her."

A small smile tugged at the corners of Tanner's lips. "I

gathered that. Tell me why you think that's problematic. If you're improving, I don't see a reason why you shouldn't attempt to open that door again."

Cameron stiffened. "Because she's not interested. She doesn't go out of her way to see me. She's not dating anyone that I can tell, but she's still going out. She's keeping her options open."

"Perhaps it's time you do the same."

He couldn't help it; he scowled at Tanner. For a moment he clenched his hands into fists, but then just as quickly, relaxed and allowed his heart to settle. It was getting easier, and that fact alone brought a small smile to his lips. "No."

"I'm not suggesting that you move on. All I'm saying is that a few dates might ease the loneliness you've been struggling—"

"I'm not lonely," Cameron cut him off. "I just… miss her. And if I can't have her, then I don't want anyone else. I can't explain it. It's like her soul spoke to mine. We belong together, and I know that in the marrow of my bones. I've never been happier than when she was mine."

Tanner nodded. "That's understandable. I suppose you have a couple things to think about then."

Cameron didn't bother asking what Tanner meant. The guy was great at expounding on what he was thinking.

"You need to get to the root of your concerns and figure out what it is that will help you overcome your triggers. It won't be easy, and change won't happen overnight. But it will help you in the future as you move forward. Then you're going to have to decide if opening the door to a relationship with Sophia is something you can handle emotionally and mentally."

Nodding, Cameron let out a sigh. "I'll think about it."

Over the next week, that was all Cameron thought about. He couldn't dredge up the courage to call his brother. They'd had a good conversation when Cameron had apologized for his behavior, but their current relationship was rocky at best. He really didn't want to tear open old wounds when Samuel didn't seem inclined to take responsibility for what he'd done.

There was an ache in Cameron's chest over that. It was like his heart had turned into a clam and Samuel's behavior was that grain of sand that irritated his insides. At some point Cameron prayed it would result in something better. But for now, he'd focus on the other side of things.

Sophia.

The more he thought about her, the more he desired to tell her everything he'd experienced from the moment he'd met her to where they stood right now. He needed her to know that he was still all in. He couldn't sit back on the sidelines anymore.

He just prayed that he wasn't making a mistake in going to her first rather than letting her come to him.

Sophia stood with two men, laughing at something one of them said. The music was loud enough that Cameron couldn't hear the topic of conversation. But from where he stood, he could see how aware Sophia was of his own presence. She had looked over at him a handful of times since he'd arrived. Based on the fact that she spent most of her evening with Emma and Emma's husband, it was clear she wasn't here on a date. No one guy had danced more than once with her. That had to be a good sign.

Cameron hovered in his own group—mostly made up of the guys who worked for Mateo. Roman was with them, too, and he nudged Cameron with a chuckle. "What are you doing over here when you clearly want to be somewhere else?"

Glancing in his friend's direction, Cameron bit back a smile. Today had been a good day. It was getting easier to see Sophia spending time with other guys—mostly because he'd been forced to observe her and had started to notice subtle differences in the way she treated them versus the way she'd treated him when they were together.

Sophia might have a natural flirty way about her, but she had no interest in anything other than friendship.

Cameron let his eyes drift back to Sophia. A question hovered on the edge of his tongue, but Roman took pity on him and answered it before Cameron had a chance to voice it.

"She still wants you."

"How do you know?" The question was quick and snapped out before Cameron knew what he was saying.

"Because you've been here a total of thirty minutes and she's been staring at you for half of them." Roman elbowed him. "Just go talk to her. What could it hurt? You're already broken up. Might as well see if there's any spark left."

Right at that moment, "She Ain't Ready" by Luke Combs came over the speakers and it was like Cameron had been transported back to that first night he'd danced with Sophia in Texas. His hands twitched and his eyes found Sophia's.

She'd noticed it too.

Without thinking, Cameron moved in her direction. Even if this was the last dance they'd ever spend in each other's arms, he'd take it. His heart belonged to her no matter what anyone else said.

Sophia's eyes followed him as he made his way to her. The men who had been talking with her were gone now, allowing them privacy to speak. But he wasn't going to be happy with just talking to her.

"Dance with me, please," he said, holding out his hand. It wasn't a question. And thankfully, Sophia didn't refuse him.

His heart pounded. His hands grew clammy. Before the words escaped his mouth, he knew what he was going to say, and he prayed that she'd accept it.

"Cameron—" she started, but he cut her off.

"I'm in love with you, Red."

She blinked up at him.

"I was in love with you from the first moment I saw you. On that first night, I'd planned on finding out where you were from so I could relocate."

"What?"

His hold on her tightened as if he was worried she might fly away. Or run. There was no going back after starting this conversation. The only way was through. "I knew that night that you were it for me. I knew that no one else would hold a candle to the feelings I had, and I... just didn't want to scare you away. I can be... intense."

She blushed, but he didn't miss the way she'd tensed in his arms. She was still holding back. And why wouldn't she? He'd not given her any indication that he'd changed. And honestly, there would be no way of knowing until she forgave him and he had a chance to prove it.

"I know I haven't earned a second chance yet," he whispered, moving closer to her ear. "I know you deserve a man a million times better than me. But he won't love you the way I do." His thumb traced circles on the back of her hand, and he refused to pull back to see her face—not until he finished what he had to say. "I hope eventually you'll find it in your heart to forgive me. One day, I hope you'll see our potential and take me back." Cameron waited, swaying with her as the song neared its end.

When he pulled back, all he could see was the conflicted nature of her expression. It even appeared that she was holding back tears.

"You don't have to say anything, Sophia. I'm not going to force you or give you an ultimatum. I simply wanted you to know that my feelings for you haven't changed. Not since Texas and not since we've broken up."

The song came to an end and Cameron released her. He left her to think about what he'd said as he moved to the bar and ordered himself a soda.

29

Sophia

"You're shaking! What's wrong?" Emma rubbed her hands up and down Sophia's arms.

"Everything. Nothing. Gah, I don't know." Sophia's eyes sought him out, searching for the man who had just laid his heart on the table. It couldn't have been easy for him to confess any of that to her, especially after she'd turned him down so many times. She couldn't believe he'd said any of it, and right now, she didn't know how to respond.

"What happened?" Emma tried again. She was giving her husband a nervous look. "Do you need me to take you home?"

Sophia's eyes landed on him then. The man who had managed to steal her heart and had kept it locked away all this time. His eyes met hers, and for a moment she thought he might charge right back over here to kiss her. She glanced at her friend as if she were her lifeline.

The worst part about that idea was that she wasn't completely against it.

Her cheeks heated, and she tore her eyes from her friend. "Cameron."

"What about him?"

The warmth in her body spread like wildfire. "He wants me back."

This time, Emma looked for the topic of their conversation. When her eyes landed on him, they bounced back to Sophia. "Okay? Is that a bad thing?"

Sophia covered her face with her hands. "No." She shook her head. "Maybe. I don't know, Emma. We weren't any good for each other—"

"Why, because he had a jealous streak?"

"Because he beat up his brother for trying to kiss me."

By the hesitant look in Emma's eye, Sophia could tell she didn't exactly feel that was a bad thing.

Sophia gave her friend a pointed look.

"Okay, okay." Emma laughed. "It wasn't his brightest moment. But seriously, you said yourself that he's getting better. You've been watching him like a stalker over the last month. He's going to therapy. He's not intervened on any of your dates. Would it be so bad to give him another chance?"

Shoulders slumping, Sophia forced herself to not look in his direction again. "What if things go back to the way they were? What if he can't control himself and I'm the trigger?" Her voice lowered into something more pitiful. "I don't think my heart could take having him only to lose him again."

When Emma didn't seem to have anything to say, Sophia

gave her a questioning look. Finally, her friend spoke. "That's a risk, for sure. But let me ask you something. Do you want to live your life in what-ifs? Because I have a doozy for you. What if he's your soulmate and this is the last chance you have to keep him before he moves on with someone else?"

The pain that ripped into her chest at that question made Sophia breathless. She glanced over to Cameron, and then her blood ran cold. The reason Emma had asked such a thing was standing right there next to Cameron.

The girl was beautiful. She had long legs, a tiny waist, and blonde hair that fell to her lower back in waves. She was Sophia's opposite in almost every sense of the word. And Cameron was smiling at her like he used to smile at Sophia.

No.

Sophia's hands balled into fists. Her own latent jealousies were attempting to break through the barriers she'd put into place with all her own hard work at therapy and strengthening her prayer life. She couldn't let Cameron slip through her fingers. Emma was right. Cameron had been doing a lot to improve himself. He'd gone to lengths that she hadn't even expected—like when he'd apologized to his brother.

What if she lost her chance with him out of fear?

"You guys have been apart long enough," Emma said. "Maybe now that you've put some water under the bridge, you'll be ready to try again." Her friend's words resonated with Sophia somewhere in the back of her mind. "No one is perfect, Sophia. Cameron's been trying. That's all you can hope for."

"What if... we're just too toxic... together?" Sophia voiced the concern without thinking.

"And what if you've both learned enough that you can build each other up instead of imploding?"

Sophia couldn't help but laugh at Emma's description and the way the visual popped into her head.

"He's seeing a therapist—on his own—without the promise of getting you back, I might add. That has to count for something, right?"

Sophia nodded absentmindedly. The more she watched Cameron with that girl, the more that pain in her chest ached. She needed to do something, or she was going to lose him. Maybe not today, but one day he'd finally decide he couldn't wait for her anymore.

Emma nudged her. "Then go tell him that you feel the same. Tell him that you know it won't be easy, but you guys can do it right this time."

Her legs moved of their own accord. Sophia flexed her fingers and shook out her hands. She could do this. Her eyes narrowed in on the way the girl touched Cameron's forearm. It was an innocent enough touch, but Sophia knew what the girl was trying to do, and she wasn't going to stand for it.

Sophia sidled up beside Cameron and wove her fingers between his before turning and smiling at the blonde. "Who's your friend, Cameron?"

The girl immediately took a step back and blushed as her eyes darted to the way Sophia held Cameron's hand. "Um... hey. I'm Amy."

"Hi, Amy. I'm Sophia." She leaned into Cameron's arm and rested her cheek against his shoulder. "I haven't seen you around here. Are you new?"

Amy shook her head. "Just visiting a friend." Her focus darted up to Cameron. "It was nice meeting you."

Sophia watched with a smug sort of satisfaction as Amy hurried away. But that smugness disappeared the second Cameron whirled on her. She'd anticipated the irritation she might find in his gaze but was surprised to find amusement instead.

"What was that?" Cameron demanded.

"I don't know what you're talking about," Sophia said airily. "I just wanted to come over here and tell you something."

His hand tightened on hers and he pulled her against him with his other hand at the small of her back. "And what is that?" he murmured near her ear, giving her all kinds of shivers.

Her words died in her throat as the reality of her situation settled on her. This was utterly terrifying—to return to something that had been both exhilarating and painful all at once.

Cameron tsked. "Don't tell me that you came over here to interrupt my conversation with that lovely young woman because you were *jealous*." Thankfully, there was teasing in his tone. Unfortunately, it did nothing to make her feel better about what she'd been caught doing. He pushed her just far enough away to meet her eyes. "Sophia, talk to me," he urged. "Don't toy with me."

Her heart did a triple backflip at the intensity with which he stared at her. She swallowed thickly and shook her head. "I'm not toying with you." Her cheeks warmed with embarrassment. "And while I'm not making excuses by any means, perhaps a little bit of jealousy is needed in some situations." She pinched her fingers together with a grimace, then held her breath as she waited for his response.

He watched her for what felt like an eternity and then threw back his head and laughed before pulling her against him. His voice hummed in his throat, and she could hear his own wildly pumping heart. "I'd have to agree with that," he growled against her ear. "You have no idea how good it felt to know that you were jealous enough to lay your claim on me." His fingers traced up and down her spine, and she shivered involuntarily. "It's been torture to keep my distance while you spent time with other guys."

She winced. Of course he'd struggled. His jealousies were more deeply rooted than her own. Part of her wondered if Sam had finally managed to tell Cameron the truth, but that would be a conversation for another time. She tightened her hold on him and exhaled. "I love you," she said against his chest. "I think a part of me has loved you for as long as you've loved me." She craned her neck so she could look at him fully. "And for the record, none of those guys I spent time with came close to comparing to you. The feelings I have for you are otherworldly."

He pressed his forehead to hers. "I know."

"You do?" she asked breathlessly.

"Yeah. I started to see the difference in the way you talked to them versus the way you talked to me. Maybe it's a little stuck up, but I knew you still cared for me. What we have? It's not easy to come by."

"No, it's not." She smiled at him, loving this feeling she had while being in his arms. Then her smile faltered, and the concern replaced his own peaceful expression.

"What's wrong?"

Sophia sighed, looking away. "What if—"

Cameron gave her a loving squeeze. "Don't do that. Don't for a second believe that we're going back to that place. I won't let it happen."

The hope he offered her flared to life brighter than she expected.

"I won't risk losing you, Sophia. I want you to know that

every single day you give me a chance, I'll make sure it's well-deserved. I'm not fixed by any stretch of the imagination. But I'm working on it."

Tears sprang to her eyes, and she flung her arms around his neck as she rose on her toes to kiss him. Somehow, she knew this promise would stick. Maybe it had been their time apart and the boundaries she had put into place when it came to his anger problems. Maybe it had been the fact that they'd both had to grow up and humble themselves to figure out what they needed. They might be a terrible match, but they were also perfect for one another in so many ways.

His lips crashed down over hers, with a desperate need. In that moment she let herself fall into him and the possibilities of what their future would hold.

EPILOGUE

Cameron

Several Months Later

"I don't understand why you're so nervous. It's been months and you guys haven't had any issues." Roman's taunting tone only seemed to rile Cameron up even more.

He shot the man a death glare. "Because Sophia has been very vocal about the fact that she never planned on settling down."

"Wrong," Roman said pointedly. "She's said she doesn't date. Not that she won't marry. You got past the hardest part. It's a guarantee that she'll say yes."

"No, it's not," Cameron insisted, fidgeting more than he liked. He'd only crossed the space to the main house because Roman had emerged from his truck and Cameron had needed someone's opinion on the ring. He should have known better than to ask Roman. First of all, he was a guy. Secondly, they hadn't started off on the best of terms.

Roman smirked at him with a quirk of his brow. "Yeah, I guess you're right. She could tell you no. Maybe you're not husband material."

Cameron's steps faltered and he stared at Roman with a gaping mouth.

The man merely laughed. "*Easy.* I don't know much, but I can see it just like everyone else. Sophia is head over heels for you. She's not going to turn you down. Not even with a ring like that."

This time, Cameron frowned at the ring. "What? Is it not—"

Roman laughed again. "You make it too easy."

Cameron nearly snarled at Roman for all the teasing. "Just wait until you fall in love with a girl and you're worried she doesn't feel the same way you do."

He folded his arms. "Not going to happen. I don't catch feelings easy. I have lots of friends. And I've been on lots of dates. The girls flock to me. But..." He shrugged. "I dunno. I just don't get the sense that I couldn't live without them." His eyes shifted as a car pulled up and a pretty, petite woman climbed out. She smiled broadly at Roman as she shut the door.

"Is that one of the women you're talking about? The ones who catch feelings for you but not the other way around?" Cameron prodded.

Roman snorted. "Nah. That's just Olivia. We've been best friends since we were kids." His brows pulled together. "She doesn't usually come all the way out here to hang, though. Usually, we meet in town. I'll catch you later." Roman jogged toward Olivia, then turned so he was jogging backward and gave Cameron a knowing look. "Text me when you get your answer. I want to know how bad she destroys you."

Cameron glowered at Roman's retreating, laughing form. He glanced down at the ring, then shoved it into his pocket. It was perfect for Sophia. She might not have picked it out, but he'd been very attentive to her over the last year or so. She didn't like gawdy. Simple and unique. That was her taste, her style. From the red streaks in her short hair to the casual clothes she preferred to wear, this ring, with its single round stone, would match her flair to a tee.

The door to the house opened and he froze, feeling her eyes on him before he turned. He'd told her he'd be here to pick her up in about twenty minutes. She was early. Or maybe she thought he was.

And he couldn't care less.

She was dressed in a simple black blouse and a pair of cut-off jean shorts. She leaned against the doorjamb and smirked at him. "Hey, handsome."

Cameron prowled toward her, his smile growing. "Hey, Red."

Sophia rolled her eyes, then pulled the door shut and headed down the steps toward him. Her eyes drifted toward where Roman and Olivia were talking, and she cocked her head slightly. He followed her attention with his own gaze as she came up beside him.

His arm slipped around her waist, and he pressed a kiss to her temple. "What are you thinking?"

"Hmm?" she murmured.

"Roman's friend? Is she... more than that?"

Sophia snickered. "No. We always thought there might be something. Mateo and me. But nothing has ever started between them. The guys she dates are nerdier. Roman's not her type."

"And Roman's type?"

She turned to him and tugged at his shirt to pull him into her. "No one knows."

He chuckled. "That's too bad. With how much he's helped, I sorta wish I could help him find the level of happiness that we have."

She glanced over at her brother. "He helped? How?"

Cameron shrugged. "I guess he's felt more like a brother to me than my own."

That had her frowning, and it caught his attention.

"What's that look for?"

Sophia chewed on her lower lip and avoided looking directly at him. "You talk to your brother lately?" She'd been asking him that question a lot over the last several months.

He and his brother had kept in contact, but nothing life-changing had occurred. "No more than usual." His heart thundered at the mention of his brother. Not today. He couldn't think about his brother with what he had planned today. "Sophia, what's wrong? Did he say something to you?"

She shook her head. "I haven't talked to him since..."

He already knew the rest of that statement. But that didn't mean that Samuel hadn't said something to her that bothered her. "What did he say?"

Her surprise and flicker of guilt were all he needed to know he was on the right track. He pulled her to him, his hands on her waist to prevent her from pulling away.

"You can tell me," he insisted. "I won't get mad."

"It really is something you should talk to him about."

"Sophia..." he warned.

She shut her eyes, then blew out a breath. "Fine. But you

can't tell him I told you. And you can't get mad. You promised."

The way his heart picked up at her words wasn't doing him any good. He was a few seconds away from calling his brother to chew him out. But then her words cut him off cold. She wove a story that was so detailed he had no other option but to believe it. His brother had made mistakes, but he hadn't intended to hurt Cameron. All those years ago, he'd tried to be the good big brother in his own way. When Sophia was done, all he could do was stare at her.

"You promised," she said quietly.

He swallowed hard, then nodded. "I'm not... mad. Not really." He was shocked more than anything. "I'm just... digesting." His brother had actually helped in a strange kind of way.

"Are you... okay?"

Cameron nodded. "Better than ever." At some point, he'd have to confront his brother over this story. He'd need to hear it straight from the horse's mouth. But right now, he needed to do something else. He flashed Sophia a smile and draped his arm around her shoulders as he led her toward his truck. "Let's head out." He gave a nod to Roman as they passed and overheard Olivia's words before climbing into the truck.

"Please? I'm desperate. I should have never told him about you, but that's where we're at."

Sure sounded like they were more than friends. Cameron glanced at Sophia, but it didn't seem like she'd heard the same thing he had. She knew Roman better than Cameron, and it wasn't any of his business what happened between him and his *friends*.

Sophia glanced in his direction as he closed the driver-side door and started the truck. She had the most adorable grin on her face—and yet it was telling. She knew something.

Cameron paused.

"What?" she laughed.

"You tell me. What's going on?"

She shrugged. "I didn't say anything."

"You didn't have to. What's going on? No secrets, remember?"

She rolled her eyes. "It's nothing."

"I know you. That smile you're wearing? It's *not* nothing."

Once again, she brushed him off. "Maybe I'm just happy. Can't that be a possibility?"

Cameron's eyes narrowed. He put the vehicle into drive and headed off. There was a fair in town, and he'd called in advance to make sure they had a Ferris wheel. Then he'd offered extra money for them to shut the ride down for a half hour so the two of them could ride it all on their own. It wasn't exactly how their first date had gone, but they both had a soft spot for the ride at the fair and he knew it would be the best place to declare his undying love for her.

The second they walked up to the Ferris wheel, he knew exactly what Sophia's smile meant. There was a large banner that had been hung to the metal rafters of the machine— and typed out in bold lettering was the word "YES."

He stopped and turned to face Sophia, finding her biting her lip and holding back a giggle. "How did you... when... who..." Then his expression flattened. "Roman."

She shook her head, taking his hands in hers. "Isabelle has a friend working the fair this year before she heads off for college this fall."

Cameron groaned. "Is nothing sacred anymore?"

Her hands tightened over his, and she hopped up on her toes to press a kiss to the corner of his mouth. "In a small town like this one? Not hardly." Then she tilted her head slightly and smirked at him. "But to be fair, you didn't have to tell them your plans in their entirety." A laugh bubbled from her throat, and it was the most delicious sound he'd heard all day. "Honestly, I don't think that I would have heard about your plans if Isabelle hadn't been worried about me. She knew I wasn't interested in..." Her voice trailed off and she blushed. "Well, not until I met you."

Marriage.

That was what she'd been about to say.

He didn't know whether to be worried or relieved at this moment. Isabelle had probably done him a favor. He didn't know what he would have done if Sophia had hesitated for even a moment once he asked her to marry him. Now the tension in his shoulders could ease. He already knew the answer to the most important question he would have ever asked Sophia in their lifetime.

"Well?" she drawled. "Are you going to ask me, or what?"

One side of his mouth quirked upward, and he lowered himself onto one knee. Gazing up at her, he knew this was the turning point in his life. From this moment forward, it was only going to get better. "Sophia, will you—"

"Yes!" she all but hollered as she threw her arms around him with another fit of giggles. Then she pressed her forehead against his. "A thousand times, yes."

***

Hello Reader! I hope you enjoyed Sophia and Cameron's love story. Up next is...you guessed it, Roman and Olivia.

Roman Palmer has been Olivia Whitten's best friend since they were kids. He's steady, loyal, and completely off-limits... because they've never been anything but friends. But when Olivia asks him to fake-date her to win over her longtime crush, everything starts to change.

What happens when pretend feelings start to feel a little too real?

Don't miss their unforgettable story in *Palmers of Copper Creek Book Three*!

Buy the paperback version of *Palmers of Copper Creek Book Three* **on Amazon! Soon, paperbacks will also be available on my store, Natalie Dean Books (nataliedean-books.com). Be sure to check there first!**

ABOUT THE AUTHOR

Born and raised in a small coastal town in the south, I was raised to treasure family and love the Lord. I'm a dedicated homeschooling mom who loves to travel and spend time with my growing-up-too-fast son.

When I'm not busy writing or running my business, you can find me cleaning house, cooking dinner, feeding our three rescue cats, trying to make learning fun and coaxing my son to pick up his toys. On less busy days, you may also find me paddling down a spring run in Florida, hiking a mountain trail in Georgia (on the rare vacation to the mountains), or enjoying a book.

If you love Natalie Dean books, you can be notified of new releases by signing up to my newsletter at nataliedea nauthor.com, where you will also receive two free short stories for signing up. Just click on the "Free Books" tab at the top and you'll be on your way!

Also, as previously mentioned, I've opened my own online bookstore and I'd love your support! As of June 2024, I'm selling my ebooks at Natalie Dean Books. By late summer or fall 2024, I should have audiobooks, regular paperbacks, large print paperbacks, dyslexic print paper-backs and signed paperbacks all available. At the request of my loyal readers, I'll also be adding merchandise, such as glasses, cups, magnets and more. So come check out my small mom-owned author business at nataliedeanbook s.com.

You can also scan the QR code below to be taken to the home page of Natalie Dean Books.

facebook.com/nataliedeanromance

9 781964 875620